I0745052

Lifeline Rule
Doug Nufer

with an introduction by
Louis Bury

SPUYTEN DUYVIL
New York City

I'm very grateful to publishers Nava Renek and
TodThilleman, to James Siena for his artwork, and to Louis
Bury for the introduction. Daniel Levin Becker, Ava Fedorov,
and Katy Masuga were all very helpful in getting me to bear
down on the demands of this book, and very generous with
their contributions to the fulfillment of the constraint.

The constraint, conovowel, was invented by William
Gillespie in 1995 for his Travelling Portmanteau Lectures,
where it first went to work as a writing assignment for
high school students. His poetry collection, written under
the name Dominique Fitzpatrick O'Dinn, *Table of Forms*
(Spineless Books, 2006) introduced me to conovowel.

à l'évadé du dédale, Perec

A Heterodox Epic

L.E. Bury

Nufer is—*Amen*—at it anew in a lively rule-based opus, a wily caper of elaborate yen. It is a fine tonic in an era so monotone. Conovowel is a rule Nufer uses as a paramedic uses oxygen: a timely poke to waken a comatose wit. As a tenet of a tome, conovowel adores agile lexical erotica, jive moves even a puritan or a rube can avow as awesome. To cite data: "Bony babes ate sugary cones of ice to likewise bid in a salivary fury to have sex." One more: "Zygote maker ability fused in every semen eke he made." Here, side-by-side cono rule begot atypical usages of a copulative lexicon, e.g.: "every semen *eke*." Vocabulary, defiled, is a rococo demon of originality.

No, more: cono rule makes a motif of an acute topic everybody faces in a life: male-female binary. Put unelaborately: sex, as anatomy, yo-yos in acolyte Dave's evocative, now-a-male-now-a-female body. Cogitate: "my sex ID eliminated any female, male/ female, bisex or asexed" as a taxonomy tag. Every category, novel elucidates, is a policeman of icy logic; every human, a fugitive paradox. Acolyte Dave's elusive gyneco-penile mutability canonizes a mazily reticulated animality, generates an open abecedary libido gala for anybody so lured: "As an imaginary hole for every male/ female to have for an erogeny fix, I was one to be nice to my men. I gave my holy hole secularity for any to have." Some bit of analysis: as a demigod, acolyte Dave lives a tenet of epicene divinity: mixed unity. Binary separates are, for a lyrical ace like Nufer, a setup one has a duty to nix, a bogus item elites use, galore, to sow a hegemony regime.

Lifeline Rule, like so many codices à la Nufer, is a nomadic epic. A simile: Dave moves as if a Sahara camel enamored of every mirage. Fate ridicules one so hopeful, alas. A catalog of a few of acolyte Dave's inane peripatetic esoterica: "to take dope like a laboratory maze rat"; exiled as a military "cadet in a catamaran unit abode"; "taken on a ride by security police to some cozy gate nobody monitored"; "I gave my vocative yo! to be put in academy robes." Every peripatetic episode cited above betides acolyte Dave before page ten. It elevates in imaginative fever on any page later on.

A final exegesis: a tome so gamesome, so dynamic, idolizes avidity like many holy men idolize god. As a literary merit, avidity focuses on apexes alone. No laxity, no so-so monotony, no supine repose. Like Dave, Nufer uses isolated one-line jokes: a "joke menu solely was a la mode cake: finale lines." One-line jokes, as a rule, favor élan, a core vigor—evade lines of a merely moderate caliber. Every banality: removed. Every "vocality by conovowel": "a bit inutile to notify so basic a jot." Utility: solace for average dudes, everymen.

Up, or in a nadir, a novel as exotic as one like *Lifeline Rule* never is average, typical. If a buyer, in a fit of asininity, desires an average derivative tome, peruse no more: polite homiletic oratory hereby recedes as inimical amid an epidemic of animate volubility. But if a buyer elates, agog, at itemized erotic asides, adores atomic anatomical oratory, loves every volatile military saga, venerates atonal opera, likes a savory recipe for asylum ale: forage for a tome no more. Nufer, a rule guru, here mobilizes a divinely heterodox amatory cinema, rotated, every vowel, on a yaw axis.

Lifeline Rule
Nufer

O Muse, relate how one man of evasive wiles
arose to face so many set afar exiles,
aged in a memory to have razed
Wilusa's edifice.

HOMER

A lifeline rule, life line-ruled or, a life line rule can in any regime be rigid as a line made by lined utility ruler. As it is unwise to let unelucidated elite policy generate power, it is ever elusively deluded or a delusive hope for any remedy to cure some rude logic of a police rebuke.

Temerity has a lure many can elude, but every man is akin in a rut, as erotic avidity defuses one's ovine duty to cede to divinity leverage. But in any case, however a regime regulates a body of amoral Onanites, it resolutely delegates a minority hegemony to some divine figure, be he (women are rare here) holy yodeler, ululater imam, or a vituperative pater/ avatar, in a move to relegate heterodox abusive caricatures of inutility to purely futile roles in asinine cabalas.

Alas, I was an amulet acolyte to Marine Base Conovowel at a time before we had to go to war. A devoted Akita karate maven, a colonel in exile, made me copy his memorized episodes of an epic in a military code meter apace his imaginary race to revise his edited erasures. If a line came to simulate not even a relative model of a valid item or image, he was elated.

"A code poses a ruse to rise not as a rose becomes arisen as a rose, but as a fake," he regaled.

I bowed. I'd ever adored any zany Zen inanity.

Heretofore, some bogyman in a naval academy deposed a debate to nominate me to Mimical Ecole Parole, yet I had a care to hide my shaky volubility. Mimes aside, mute note-taker amulet acolytes are wary to refuse limelit arena pyromanic oratory, to favor a more refined oral agility.

We were to resume his opus, as an obese baritone veteran, agog in a haze, merely tired, or in a sedative repose, came to faze Colonel Ahi.

"Sir! I've disavowed a recon unit on a lemonade run. United Arab Emirates are my demonic anemic enemy men. An enema has an enemy nature, but I can be how I can be, for Ali, Kali, Saxony."

To him Ahi doled a, "Relax, it is over," as in a low aside to me he mused, "A veteran is a lonely he-man."

"Are we not alive? My dunes are wet as a pit a marine navigates, as if a lake were water of a like to defy verisimilitude."

"Here, here," Colonel Ahi saluted in rote lip amity.

"Do we deter or are we done for? I dare salivate for a fate to be. Time's up."

"I define fate, Marine-san. It is a job of one to decide so vital a limit as a lifeline. Time's up is one lexical usage to finalize literality."

"Can a tuna can a tuna?"

Manitoba toker, Alameda coker, or Arizona sot, a man agog in a fog of abuses is a Babelite to rile meditative natures. I cogitated awarely to be sure, but a wily wit is a facile con. I did imagine him as enured, awake yet in a daze.

Colonel Ahi ceded a nod. As a laxative cures a body of a parasite colony, his executive face made colonic a visage to repel a likely toxin.

In a fit of irony, his agitator aped a saner image to make his exit.

"If a by-law iterates a royal id to give vocality to base desires, I'd imitate docility to bow a low olé for a matador on a dare to honor an ego to win a superego legitimacy."

*

My genesis as an amulet acolyte began in a casino. Here many ran amok on a yen, a desire to tame savage nemeses in a game like dice, keno, poker, et. al. On a bet one manager of a QED utility nature made to deduce how a yen operated, an ad (in a magazine novice literati cited as "awesome") solicited a cadet unit of evocative venality. Likely delegates in a line to hone desire were to be given a new elixir, a tonic I saw as a cure for any malady. To take dope like some laboratory maze rat? O.K., I was on it.

An operative hired a rare few as amulet acolyte novice mates. In a ceremony to honor us, a titular elite gaveled one rap of a leveraged amen; a notary came to relate how, as a doxy for an exotic opera can evaginate tunes every man imagines are his alone to savor as uterine notes of a love to have, we were to manipulate loser epitomes of avarice to lose more. To be given an ability to do so, we were to be tutored in amulet evocative lore. Somatic, emotive, libidinal, or oracular eligibility made some types emit a fume nobody but an ace hole diviner of an elevated acumen eremite did educe. To some wise wizened or aware nose, haze hovered over an amulet, one defined as any body to betoken a nexus of exuded awe to set or abet a bet. Exuded awe, lore had it, emanated in inanimate waves, as an amino helix enate code to give some wary casino denizen an in of a tip.

As ewes emit a serene lobotomized amorality, we were made to be copacetic, in a move to beware to catalyze no radical elevator/ arena music. I fixed a gaze to focus on a zone removed afar or, at any rate, not at anybody.

"To babysit a Gila gator, one cajoles in italic irony," my tutor, an ex-editor, elucidated.

It eliminated a dire care, somehow. I dedicated a melody to some no-name caveman in a facile homage to base manic agony. To repel evil asides, aborigine rites of apology manytimes likewise raged in a decorum of a facile docility. "Bid aloha," gave notice repetitively to me to be serene, to fuse binocular aves of every come/ go. For in a casino, some were gone before many came. However anybody did exit or open a gate, my role was ajar. I had a definite yet animated onus of use to peruse faces. I became finer at it, as a tidy many were similar: I rose to demote several as average dupes of avarice.

But in a rare bit, an episode began. An episode was any memory to forebode more to be memorized in a later episode.

He was a military man, I noted, in a tunic of any zone, depot, or ukase regime, but it isolated one to don it as a sage to revere savage power, even if a xylem of ivy tower academy rigidity gave him a morale to defy fidelity to moronic oxen or average beverages. As agile demi-nude women of anatomy roved in a barefaced usage to give so many doses of elixir as urine can eliminate, he refused. Nobody refused as he did, in a wave to demur as if in a move to ratify nihility.

He came to bet. As a cynical operator opened a gate for a human exodus awarely to deliver everybody to some level of a module mired in a severe futility, pit epoxy wisemen acutely fixed every game. But a gamer of icy tenacity developed a positive negative to win as one won in any fix of a rig.

Enate to basic ability to defy fate were bona fide generative haled ahas! (a haled aha! was a fanatic aha! some muses emit or elicit). In a muse role now, I made my haled ahas! a halo to hover in an image to mimic a luxury pot of ore. For a haler of a halo to deliver a deluxe pot, an elixir on ice sanitized an amulet acolyte. To purify me in an oxygen ozone zone, demi-nude men of atony gave me serum.

In a lit élan, I devised a volatile laser amicus of a sure wager avowal. It acutely lacerated avocatory debate to deter a bet. At one buxom aha!, he delivered an economic ahem in a pile.

"Ducat one mil on eleven."

As a wager, it elicited a wide notice. Was it a side bet on a rotated axis by name of Axis of Omen or a major operative run on an ice cube dice game hereby? He posed as a bicipital animal of a desire to be fed. In a salivary maw of a ruminated idyl, a dice bite favored a seven or a six, as enumeravores of eleven ate rarely. For a bite cud on a rotated axis, eleven arose more rarely. Many more won by hit on a regular itinerary before digit eleven aced a pot.

"Are we to cover an Axis of Omen amen or a cubed amen?" a pit educer evoked a finality.

My military deputy wavered, as if in a daze to decide, but any daze was a ruse.

"Bipolar, at one motive. Dimeter, in a literary line."

So he, to cover, opened an adit of a mine to more of an ore lode. He divided one pile to set up one more pile to give to side-by-side games, in a time to make do.

"Resume games," a bejeweled emir evoked a finality bid.

Axis of Omen executed a rotary voyage to make some numeral an elater of one fate feted.

A delegate, given a sinecure for an ability he secured

as a dice manipulator, educed a cubed exegesis in a logic of ebony dot on ivory face: five/ six: eleven.

"Ah," a serene nod exuded a hope for a huge delivery. Minipot in, at a rate to cover a visa to Canada, he gazed upon Axis of Omen as it agitated on, ever at a more deliberate pace.

Before dynamo demise set in, a peg atop enumerated every rotated aloha by ratatat of a gone yet iterated itinerary. Come for one more time, rotary rider, every man on a bet on a numeral ago vowed, in a mute futile hope to beg. Every man aside, my motivated operator exuded a meditative serenity. But a vocalized ado got avid as Axis of Omen abated a decisive gyre.

"Go baby go!"

"Come to papa, son of a bit—"

"I got it, I got it, I got it."

Adipose cupidity puled in an atonal unison.

"Eleven," eliminated everybody but one.

"Tora tora tora," he reveled, in an enate salute.

We bowed in amity to relate to Japanese nativity. He bowed in a polite ceremony to cajole nobody. So none but a bigot or a sore loser agonized at a fate hereby given in a rotated episode.

His ore lode now evoked Eden, as in a paradise to go forever. As a caged abacus operator agilely totaled a huge pile to remit in one deluxe delivery to him, an executive bade me to come to his isolated abode.

My tenure was at a nexus of exile, he joked.

I made some recuperative jibe, but it ate no Beluga, let alone came to rehabilitate me for any sin I did. Apologize to cut a pat exit? Apology was a motive for uxoricide.

Posed on a level above me, he gazed a minute before he resumed.

"Are we not united, on one same side, in a basic epidemic of edacity?"

Civility paraded in every tic on a face beveled in age lines. Even if I made his age to be degenerate, he behaved unawarely manic as a bug.

"Imagine, to humor an executive for a bit. I've hired a camera to take valid images. A camera—not a cameraman. It operates as it is used. I've hired an acolyte cadet, an acolyte—not a maven. It or, if I care to revise, *he* can operate to do some job as use decides. A job, as in a basic utility. Here we desire but one type visitor: AB: a donor. A win is a lure to dole some tale to bare how anybody can win. An acolyte, however, is a lure for a loser. As an acolyte, none dare let anybody win."

"If a casino has every game fixed, it is a fate to lose. Can a negative tabulated eraser of overage become positive? Later, everybody loses. A win is a yo-yo, no? Can an acolyte not abet a bet of a win at one game to begin a yo-yo type hope? Hope's a rope to dupe some loser. I'd exuberate, not abuse, to begin a game."

"Debates of unilateral operative modes are not

iterated in a debut arena."

My debut in a casino role was on a towed ice wafer on a July delivery to Panama. But I had one more cake to bake.

"So, how are we to define yen?"

"A yen? A Sino capital unit."

As a definitive piñata poke detonated a finite wide focus on a finality to vary not a bit unawarely, he waved an exit open. I rose to be taken on a ride by security police to some cozy facility gate nobody monitored. An ironic aside bade me sayonara.

*

"My name José Jiménez," evoked a decades-ago comedy bit a macaw in a cage by my domicile renovated in a tone to give no nod at any Mexican origin or abuse. Somebody Dana did it, in a televised elegy for a bygone hilarity. So now at a time removed, as a loco loro raved on, a palaver of iterated inanity made me revisit a joke nobody liked, evoked in an eponym.

A visitor, a non-U.S. American of a name José, has a desire to go to pelota games. A big one comes up on a date he decides on in a minute, but a populated arena, sated in a cozy-to-capacity volume, can abide by not one more fan. A pole, however, is one locale some daredevil ace can use to top, in a move to bare his agility. So, he gives it a go. By rope, he moves up, up, up, above humanity, til on an apex. At a time before game time, here rises a rayon American icon on a rag of a cerise red, ivory pale, navy but azure decor of a mode to betoken a fidelity to native solidarity. In a loyal unison, everybody faces up, in a ceremony to serenade: "José can use sí . . ."

Now in one tenor of analogy, my life was up a pole. But, I had a solo rote line by some Aves of a renegade—no serenade by any populace—to regale me. So repetitive were his unabated one-sided odes, I had a desire to vacate my home. To move to some more homelike locality, many get a job.

As it arose, my cumulative positives of ability were few. Educated as an amulet acolyte? Sure. To be more fit in eligibility for a job, I decided on an academic usury bid. I gave my vow in a vena cava desire to go to Hyde Naval Academy, to recapitulate my cadet utility.

To secure my vow, a military sales executor elucidated a benefit itinerary. Navy bases of operative forage were located in exotic, even Utopic, arenas: Italy, Delaware, Mexico, Babylon, Azores, Okinawa, Cadiz, Aruba, Yukon, Iraq, Iran, Oregon, Oman. A cadet in a catamaran unit abode can examine paradise, become visitor of every bona fide fun Eden, amuse many women or any man as an amore, he related.

I gave my vocative yo! to be put in academy robes. A lime kepi made me pine to win a tomato beret of a rated ace, for in any military role, we covet a mode/ color epitome, to be put above basic utility level. In a fever of inane temerity, my fury decided.

"I have to become pilot of an Avocet, a mariner of a jet."

"An axon exam is an agility caliper. If anybody so put upon, in a wire fiber ire, can use his anatomy to defer atony, he evades eliminated anonymity."

"So, fame comes as a sure rebate to anybody so honed as an axon axe?"

"Not at one time. Before fame can cohere some fine repute, here comes an alary monitor, a pod of axolotyles in one ravaged exile menace for a dire diner at a remote coyote site, several ur or Eve watery body mirages an Adam awarely navigates. A pilot is one to simulate many voyages in an exam ecology."

"So be my fate."

*

Basic ability pedagogy was a savage developer. An evil abecedary tutored us in an agony to dehumanize: how one can abide japes of acetylene, butane, calamine, decibel, edema, fire, gore, hives, irony, juju, kamikaze, lobotomy, melody, nip, origami, pare, Qena, ridicule, Simonize, telekinesis, USO, vise, Watusi, xylo, Yuletide, Zapata. To be given a carapace, we were repetitively bedeviled. I hate to be bored in a game nobody can elucidate, let alone to be solely bare to damage, but unanimity somehow inanely did atone for abuses, if everybody got abused as one.

Later, I merely got over it. A filed (or is it a defiled?) enamel of an abominated origin enured us. I capered in an anabatic idyl, above base cares, as I was elevated on a vapor of elated amity.

To get us animated in a camaraderic asininity, parade rites acutely resonated in a hi-lo pitapat I revisited as a cub ode for a den unit in a hike caravan.

"One to-"

"Bite me."

"Five to"

"Hate me."

"None to tolerate me."

"To do!"

"To do."

"To be."

"Not or."

"A be to not."

"Or a to be-"

"To be!"

Later a degenerate parody developed in a levity to rebuke military banality, but at a core, we were loyal.

Academy time did operate to go by. Before we were solid or in any capacity to be fit, an exam of a finale came to separate many loser ovine types. I had a hope to be cut. Any pilot ego vapidity had evaporated. I merely desired an exit, a new academic arena. So, to be sure to be demoted, I made a move to sabotage my exam. Any jot I put on a line was an item of a fakery to befit a moron.

A typical exam aside was a focus on esoterica. To wit: "If one decimates an enemy, how are we to decide damage? By times a decimal of a dot-one? By some huge totality to defy an abacus? Or is an enemy forever an enemy, never one to be done?"

My native renegade deposed: "An enemy is a ten over one pal, a mate for a decade. To decide some decimal is a to-do for a dodo to do. Damage, herefore, reduces at a rate gone minus of a ten over one times a decimal of a dot-one."

My tabulator ability made havoc of a hokum. Above my wily ludic exegesis, I nominated a caricature to be me, by some name like my name. Not an eponym, as an eponym is ever used in a regular arena: my moniker in a code here became some vocalic ibidem in a tome page line to be like my moniker as it is: one Bare Bosom (a.k.a. Dave Dolor).

A panel of anonymity met in a move to decide my fate, name, moniker. I later awoke to how it abated. Even if it operated as an abusively made funicular utility line to defy dynamic elevated use, somehow it elucidated a veracity. My new academic arena came to be Mimical Ecole Parole, by capitulated unanimity. Some facility bogyman I cowered at, as a natural acidity made me gag, in an agile gyre saw I was a code cadet of a rare type: somebody to be made to deliver a ruse coded in a parole to redefine how a tome page line defines.

*

A new, atypical, erudite pupil abided at Ecole Parole. Not a savage duty dupe, but a refined ace was one more likely to be here. Yet an animal of a cadet, as one made by military regimen, I had a bodily vigor of ability to rebuke my mates as a tiger abuses a lemur, if any came to ridicule me. But a majority gave me no notice. Some were lonely, however. I had a sideline to babysit a few of an eligibility for a cute pity.

My generosity made me popular, as a fine many saw I cared, even if I merely was enamored of a manipulative capacity for one to take care to begin a mutiny. Not a mutiny to take MEP over in a literal usage, but a mutiny to be a pure model of an agitated amenity. Power of one to generate power, in a revised isogamy, was a base care to make me care for anybody for a care take sake.

My motives I hid, as one tutored in amoral agility can ape doges of a legitimate morality to hide his amorality. So to fit in, I put in a time to divine basilica duty for a devoted eremite pater in abase humility robes. In a linen of a holy manure, he bade me to bow. I did, in an ave to be demure. He was elated. I gave him a dime to be sure. He was agitated. I vowed a bit of a labor in an acolyte capacity.

"An amulet acolyte capacity?"

My résumé was an agape file. Some domino catena Babelite teletype made me to be liberal, as if I were to have given a Japanese military man a tip in a magic oracular avowal. Any basilica had use for a cadet of amulet acumen.

"I, Peter, a Pater above Hades aside Jerusalem over anybody, hereby give ye to come done ken, a wire to be tuned in, aware," he raved a seminary vow of a ceremony to venerate divinity mates.

I let on as if I were ripe to be taken as an acolyte to be his imaginary casino mate, so he let on I was owed an exit. I ate my wafer, a wad of a filo, made some genu-posited ave Mary for a holy role.

"Be gone," he bade me to be done.

"So be bygones," I emulated a mitered elite, to recover a bit of a leverage to manage to debate.

Not a minute later, one more rumor amused a cozy few: I had abused an elevated avatar in a defamatory game to no sure care nor exonerative finality.

*

My Mimical Ecole Parole life became reticular in one more mode: heterosex. A love sorority came by to levitate for an anabatic elemi vapory caper of an aroma to make men agog. In a bosomy la-ti-da hiya melody, a come-by gave notice to jejune males of a bid on a dare to copulate. Bony babes ate sugary cones of ice to likewise bid in a salivary fury to have sex. As I was an animal of an age of eligibility to mate, my nature motivated. I made time every minute to meditate sexily.

Some regular acolyte, cadet, or average male can evocatively pine for a nubile body to take for a ride, but an amulet acolyte has a power in a meditative mode to be telekinetic in a focus of emanated use for a vagina fit. I was, I saw, alone by din of any decibel of a focused ability, facile to be telekinetic. Or, as a paradox of a relative logic opined, any desires I did emanate were definitely set in a resonated Eden every woman of an age to mate had an iron uterine wire to tune her id of Eve to.

So here we were: me, my male waves of erotic ozone, many females of a positivity to be wet in a yen of a zone for a comely me to pet amid an aridity to rile many more wary males of a foregone care to covet. I had a native timidity to limit any racy he-man oratory. Limited, I made my bovine libidinal ability jut as a Bozo nose to cower a merely rude man. As a lure to make women avid, a timidity limit is a very wily wile for a male to wage. Banal apes evoke libido power in a defecated irony, but an amulet acolyte delicately can eliminate many a vile habit a male poses.

I, herefore, had a bit of a to-do to defuse. So many nubile women adored an imaginary me to have for a mate, my popularity became Casanovan. I behaved in a polite nobility to sate desires of any female to come to me. To make love to do so, my libido faded, even if I manipulated in a mode to simulate by labile, digital, or anal idyl a copulated analogy. So posited a generosity made me a bucolic enamorata, but a bubonic epidemic of abuse by overuse severely put a cap on any levity.

To relax, I retired. I became not an eremite, but a vicar in Pete's ave Mary basilica.

*

Sometimes, a favorite basilica duty, female bikini pubic odor, or avocatory bake sale delicacy had a lure to divide my focus. I did agonize to become educated in every parole code to be made mimical.

Of every code, however, one came to take me by vise bite love for a dynamite panegyric oratory: conovowel. I vowed, in a ludic amity, to major as an erudite pupil in a conovowel academic arena. To cite but a few operative bonuses a conovowel usage gives: evocative levity, cumulative volubility, relative celerity, limited opacity but open imaginative tenacity; to cite but a few usages a conovowel user is aware to recapitulate: zygote, Vatican, isotope, cacuminal, oxymoron, ivy, honorificabilitudinitatibus (if, as a valid oral unit of any parole, honorificabilitudinatitibus is agape to debate, so devises a Wikipedic usage ((to cite *Lose Love Labor*, A. five, S. one, before "Honorificabilitudinatibus: A

Sonata" by Dom. O'Din, aka Wily Giles, arose to define conovocality)) lexicon I go by, but I cede to some Ox.E.D. ace to disavow it as a valid unit, as I do not opine to define so polymeric an anomaly). At any rate, conovowel is a code to dare. Basic in a hetero set of a rule yet esoteric in use, conovowel uses a relative few adobes in a race gone zany to put up a hut. As a model, it evoked a figurative vitality to vary, rotate, modify by many gyres any set I devised. I herefore dedicated a fanatical avidity to meditate, cogitate, nominate, ratify, validate by my waves of a nature to vary. By wit or a wiles utility, somebody tutored in a rut of a rote can unawarely get any code.

Some decided a code was a device to tame feral originality. To be fixed in a code was a fix one can use to be liberated in a derivative sinecure to copy— not originate. But I saw a device like conovowel as a developer of original opuses, as it evoked an agility to be lucid in a new or unused operative vocality.

So I gave my tenured educator elites a rare bid. I focused on a major of a very limited evocative capability. Some did aver I had a puny positivity to levitate my rated academic average to be so put in a pit of an arena; many more had united in a move to decide my vanity, temerity, jejune fever, or unaware nature motivated a dive to some nadir of a no-win exit. Anyhow, it evoked a fen of an academy mire nobody had ever exited.

I, herefore, was a pupil in an ecole parole put on a

sole parole: to become levitated, I had a tome paper on a conovowel usage to do for a final exam, a take-home paper exam. A lazy none-for-anybody dynamic amused everybody, yet as a time came to define my literal ecole parole rules of academic eligibility for a rise to be let go, none led. Or, I was amazed in a daze to bet I had a liberality to revise how a tome can operate. Were notes a rule? Were cited erudite tomes of ivy tower elites a bonus or a minus? Originality was a hot academy topic, as a debate did arise to pare how it evaded everybody to be noted as original. Or, to make now an opus anybody can awarely set as a new item, isolated as one, sole, novel item, imagined in a fit of unilateral aha! was atypical. An original opus of a type to give more lore, data, hip or even a wise lucidity to some topic or arena, for a general utility, benefit, or a sake to develop an ever aware maturity likewise was, I deduced, an erudite model in a degenerate disuse.

So, my paper, in a move to be novel, I saw as a novel. As I exited, I got an elusive rebuke to be timely, but a negative lot of any regulatory nature to do more. No more but a page limit unenumerated, a dare to make my total on a conovowel axis, anyhow, in a novel I'd imagine, so to mimic.

*

I got a validated exile visa to be solitary, to give me more time to do my paper. A solitary pupil evaded every regular ecole seminar or academy regularity to focus on one topic. As a bonus, I was eliminated as a regular ecole pupil. In one conovowel arena pit, an academy rule came to bury me, to separate me. So severe were my regimes, it abated any tutored ecole benefit, in a paradox of a laboratory to defy pedagogy.

My solitude, however, isolated alone solely my conovowel analysis. I yet abided amid a colony. Put upon as a satyr or adulated as an amulet, I was one popular amigo.

"Dave, can I take notes on a few usages of a conovowel esoterica?"

Peter elaborated an elaborate panorama to secure his awakened avarice to visit a coded ecology. Holy lore was a repository for a code to decode. To wit, it elucidated a wily many parabolic episodes. As a pater in a basilica, he had a duty to rarefy but edify. To do so, he had a literary care to refine literal analysis in a hope to deliver an anagoge. To solicit a favor I had an ability to do, he gave me some holy tale to recapitulate by conovowel. I gave him a logical anagogical opus.

I hereby deliver it.

A family man of a desert abode, Kale, had a tabula rasa voyager in a fine toga come to him as if in a mirage, for a halo corona gave his awesome visitor an eligibility to be holy. So Kale posed a holy role meter of operative humanity to verify. "Have some rare camel igidi," he bowed as a lazy susan of every delicacy rotated a bite to be taken. Solely some holy man (or a god) is one to refuse camel igidi, he figured. Aha! Lo but a negative nare wary tic of a nose gave to refuse. "Sip a kefir of a beverage finery," he waved at a siren in a sari to deliver a cup of elixir. One more time, he refused. In a lucidity taken as a cover of avarice, Kale decided a god owed any man a favor, if a man, in amity, made to give more for more. For one more lure, he bade, "Take my Jezebel as a wife for an idyl." "An idyl?" a positive note colored a foregone "Yes!" In a move to be sure, Kale defined idyl as, "A labor of a lover." In a finale to define him as a fake, not a fakir, a nod abated any more debate. Now, as a family man of a desert abode, Kale was a sire of a foxy many nubile women by beloved Eva. None had a name Jezebel. One by one gave solely her anonymity by a "Not I" to deny him. At a minus of one to love, he made move to go, but a hale Kale gave him one more hope to be sated. "In a side facility, one can adore Jezebel as a wife," he led. In a rage to be given a wife, his awesome visitor alit upon a homely domicile for an animal. A sexy he-haw of an onager, in a desire to be had, exuded an aroma to sate men in a mule rut.

"Anagoge, my vile vicar! A cynosure to lure some pure rube to luridity," Peter orated on as I made my final exit.

*

Eliminated as a vicar, I became more secular. I yet exuded an amulet oracularity, so to be a jocular oracular amulet of a rake was a move made by my very nature. To be jocular, I did a comedy set as a sometime comic. As a facility, conovowel usage was a joke, many did aver. I, however, avowed a desire to develop ability in every lucidity zone conovowel opened.

I began at a cabaret on a mic open eve for anybody to give some gag a go. Sometimes I had a care to do "My name José Jiménez," or a mime tale, but as everybody before me got abuse for average humor, I had a dare to do more. Bad, even, if I were to decide, rated over average.

So, I did an analysis. I saw a model a joke made, by how it exited on a finale. My cure was one to cut. If a finale line was a focus of every joke, my joke menu solely was a là mode cake: finale lines.

As it is, it is a was.

I never ate to be fat.

I wipe my paw on a sofa.

How abused?

I put 'em in a recipe to make police.

But if one has one, can one run it?

Am I some developer?

I can open a sideline?

How I can hereby make my salary?

Velure! Cut ------elure-------!

Here's one we never use.

Nice to get a fine made pot o' java.

Bu-bu-bu-wa-wa-wa-wa-di-di-da-dove-do?

Some finer average delicacy, no?

Yet it is a so tiny bit of a bite to have.

So puny for a tiger of a bony hide—he's a baby to be fed!

Aha, later a Malamute gives up.

Abe? No job or ability, but O to him I'm a god.

Is anybody he dare tip?

Or a bow in awe to my fine humility?

He never ate before.

How are we to make some gale?

Huh? Amid a fire sale?

Civility's aces!

Everybody's in *one* locale.

No lady: my wife.

Redo, redo, redo.

To define so purely.

Decades of a love to beg.

If I get a tiny base rate, ya have lower of a debit if I give no remit.

As a solace bonus, a remunerated in every mode deluxe voyage for a many more dates' exile to Cape Canaveral.

As I delivered every line, more here tolerated it. Or, at any rate, none javelined any japes in a move to ridicule me. But a wary solicitude resided as evocatively my lines elicited an unawares, even a polite, docility. No sonic asides of any type let on if anybody got it. I had an oxymoronic ability to rivet as I bored, I came to hope. My nonemotive yet emotive delivery had a retired or an aged opacity capacity to repel as it abusively lured. I was a mimic of a time-honored operative type done by many, but a type done many decades ago. Nobody here was even alive for it as it operated, in a cabaret or a musical, a gala for a holy secular edit iterated in a memory, revisited in a love for a time forever in an era to be done for as it is.

As it is, it is a was.

*

"Are we here to have some fun, as in, am I to be disabused or . . . used?"

"I notice how a babe can emanate mojo jam, as I give her a sip of a love mojito."

"How is a so fine to pine for as a dynamite xylemite like yew alone? Sap is on a rise to bury my tulip in a bowery."

Many times in a bar I sat alone to monitor as a male parade made moves on every female to come by. Pity made me deliberate how I'd evaded a likewise fate. To have to beg inanely for anybody to take notice was a run of a savage humility no rat ever agonized over, as it awarely navigated in a maze to get a bit of a Romano.

"So, babe, hop a ride to my paradise pad."

One kamikaze was an ace. His amore line was a lazy, care-liberated I-got-it. If a lady gave her evasive rebuke to his inane polo poke, he faked a soporific, "Aloha," to mimic a jet of enema hosed ah, or a catatonic "Oh, a loser." On average, no line was a surefire lure. Was a zany rap a ceremony to make women adore moronic apes or, as I came to deduce, were my men of a tame type, solely busy in a rite to defy men?

As I sat on a side, to take care to behave politely, comely women of utility came to deliver any doses of elixir I'd elicit. A rare few isolated ewes educed a diminutive dose (not unawarely to be set up as a monopoly gamer amid a ram of a rod economy). But even an isolated ewe mimed a pule to puke to deny my rival oxen of a bovine wit.

I had a go to reduce my natural amulet evocativity, to be demure. But as I retired, I did emanate waves of a gonad ad, a notice for a genital exuberater any lady can use. Not everybody, but a solitary woman of utility became riveted in a focus of awe to be delicate to me.

"Have some dates of a Jerusalem agora," her amity gave me vibes, as if a wave by me met a wave her uterus emanated in a fix of a mix.

"I like bites of a date. So very nice for an item." My pixy nip itinerary made her aware how I devote my Yoga like tenacity to saliva duty. Duty? No job I'd adored ever ate so beloved a date.

"How are we to make dates evoke time to come?"

"Do we dare to revisit a memory to revise how it is as it is in a new episode?"

We were, to cite some saw, on a same page. Coded in a rife conovocality, we had a lot of esoterica to bat upon in a refinery move to reduce raw abalone to edibility. But it opened a gate to more to do.

"My name's Amana."

"Mine, Dave."

We bowed as I gave her a hug. An agile hug, it emulated a foregame mates use to become hedonic. I put a pet upon a hip, as I let a pet of a pat of a forage by her evoke my rise.

"My time here's over at eleven," Amana gave me hope for a luna sonata coda to my bar idyl.

"I barely can emanate how avid I am as one to tabulate so many minutes."

*

Amana had an atypical ago lifetime to relate. Her era model of a juvenile lifeline code was enate—not of an academy modality. Her enate nativity mama was a papa, by bi-sexed vivacity. Her enate nativity papa was a mama, likewise. Conovowel as a mode to live by came by natural operative run, as anybody developed in a home so bipedaled is one (was one?) to depose.

To have native capability to cajole by conovowel awed anybody not a native to so rigid a regime. My code to codify made me super avid in awe to her agile, labile cacuminal usages.

I had a care to dare to be met, as I was examined in a debut Amana set up, at a locale by her enate Mama/Papa's abode: Café Pelo Pole. Mama had on a wig of a calico hive bun, as a corona to top a robe cape. Papa had on an A-line camisole mini-bodice his agape pajamas owed an apology to. Not of a wit or a care to be fine, Papa digited a mucusy nare bit. I relaxed. A woman of utility came for a menu note, so we gave her a basic amenity rebus of an ovulated exegesis aside bacon, a caramelized anise cake, ham, a do-nut, olives, Americanos. A non-oral ave by lined-in-ebony figures of a basic imagery did it, as any vocality by conovowel is a bit inutile to notify so basic a jot.

"Amana vocalizes a love for an academy man."

I was aware how a conovowel user is one to be barefaced. I herefore bared an ace to face Papa.

"My love for Amana can abide no rival. I hereby vow I capitulate never." As I so deposed, I saw I had an ironic Alamo tenacity to my tone.

Mama gave me her Amazon, "Ahem," a pirana jaw opened in an acerose humor. "A man Amana manages is one to defy. But a man in an academy . . . can a pupil of an academy have power?"

"If I have to generate power as a dynamo, no, but

anybody can use some fuse."

By home rule rite, time-honored in a rage to dominate me, Papa/ Mama diced a potato viz-a-viz a future son-in-a-law of a family man. Anybody to be posited as a mate for Amana was one to be metered, as any Papa/ Mama made do to vet in a move to debar any rude savage, fake duke, bum, or abuser.

I gave my polite, nicety-rife recital in an evasive waver. A tide rose to recede to deliver a hazed itemized A-B-A fare, to become some similar agitative regime to depose to me by set of a Do/ Do Not avowal of operative law. As Papa gave Do rules in a rale, Mama gave Do Not asides in a pule.

"Do make water, as it is a bodily luxury to be rid of urine."

"Do not adore new abusive vices as iceboxes in a fire."

"Do venerate gas of a defecative nature."

"Do not eliminate mud as a cure."

"Do reposit a taken item as a donated amenity."

"Do not execute."

"Do covet a name for a vanity case."

"Do not evade."

"Do verify."

"Do not exonerate celibate heresy."

"Do get even as a remedy."

"Do not agitate merely to defy."

"Do mutilate rebate doles of a federal executive

generosity."

"Do not edit a codex of a memory."

"Do remove by law any tag on a sofa."

"Do not imagine some typical epode."

"Do devise to make new episodes."

I gave my yes as a bit of a nod as I bit a bacony bite. Papa was a busy man in a do-nut epic of a no hole bar. Amana had an olive, Mama ham. A future family fete hereby purulated in a pus opus of a dined idyl. Every time my future family mates ate to make some ceremony to give homage to holy, secular, or any natal aloha, we'd opine to be dehumanized in a net of a reticulate debate. Do/ Do Not olives or exam oregano were to cover every salad. One-sided asides of a top (age-before-nubility) to lower a dynamic of unilaterality did exonerate nobody. We were fated.

*

Every few eves, a note came by wire, telex, or e-fax as ozone let it in on a file to my Mac. Amana had operated it as a device set in a conovowel edited usage, so my delivery lines of utility to bases of a remote locale were limited in a regime to dedicate me more to my code. To revise by radical edit of a code made some notes evoke damage done by rumor, as a finale bore solely some rare bit of a similarity to how it originated.

E.G., one by some venality con:

Aloha Madam, Aloha Sir:
Open a gate to paradise! Honolulu has every civilized amenity, but a bonus of a savage habitat is a mere bit afar, in a colony for a malady.
Colonize Moloki! Save humanity! Dedicate time to pet a leper!
As one honorary care giver, anybody can abide to reside by fire coral, azure water, in a sun enameled Eden of utopic ecology. For a tidy sum of a tiny remunerative total, anybody has an imaginary locale to vacate to, some deluxe home like nobody's in any Dakota hole.
Make We Care Colony Moloki so validated a home for everybody!
For a time limited on a timely basis, an operator is on a duty to put every
woman, every man in a paradise colony.

More were not as inanely lame:

Policy Securer:
An acute salary rise for executives above rated rate has unilateraly made coverage for any vital anatomy care capitulate to capital overage.
So to take safe care to make sure we're secure, we have taken a liberality to remove some rare coverages a few (if any) have to beg us in agony to give.

To wit: anybody to have now or anybody to have had anytime before: hives, edema, beri-beri, bubonic uremic abuse, melanoma, curare toxicity, defecative debility, epidemic edacity, fever or a coma, some fetus or a hematoma, genital ivy, some hex of a hepatic or a hematic epidemic, a hip of inoperative senility, bad ovary utility, rabid animality, renal anility, or any pox of a hope to be cured is a loser.

As ever, everybody's a care for us.

In apology,

Medicate Surety Co.

But a vile many were:

New Unit in Unity

Yo! Come papa to mojo da virility con una mama lode like some big ox!

A new unit in unity can amaze, so every date's a lady daze.

Surety rate hike, come-get-it erotica virus, or inane sales ave: rarely did any note make me take time to remedy some bit I had an ability to fix. In a majority, to take no notice was a wise hem of a haw. A rare note did agitate me to decide, however, if I had an axe to wag in a parade to debate some vaseline validity.

Ten ut!

It is a duty, honor, epitome to be military. We have noted an acute degeneracy w/abuse to military mobility re: Cadet Amulet Acolyte Dave Dolor.

A veteran is of an eligibility to be put in an ecole parole forever, if ever it operatively be, but a cadet is of an ineligibility to defer a duty to honor a duty to be military.

Herefore, to be mobilized, it is a fate for one Dave Dolor as iterated above to go to Marine Base Conovowel, as an Amulet Acolyte for one Colonel Ahi.

Some few of a power as a marine! Fe fi fo fum, of one for everybody done!

Verily,

General Ipole

*

To be taken afar as a marine was an exit I came to like. For one major item, it agilely removed a duty to be wed a.s.a.p. As a paradox, it exonerated a caricature Papa/ Mama made me model as a manikin of a Ken: an academy man as a hedonic abuser, a nabob of unexamined ability. Military life gave me time to get a résumé. However I had emulated any type hero was inutile to Papa/ Mama: to develop, one had a duty to do more. But above more, to be taken as an operative to Marine Base Conovowel as an amulet acolyte to Colonel

Ahi was a move for any conovowel user, educated or enate, to put at an apex of a juvenile's imaginary rise.

Juvenile? My cadet age was upon a time not over. Imaginary rise? No top of any juvenile's apex of a rise was a verity before he was enameled in a fire cure. Fire cure? Some rules of a military conovowel unit I came to live by came later, as I came late to tabulate how operatively huge my coded arena was. A military base was a sole bit of a zone so ruled. I saw it as a definitive race typed unit, a lot of humanity to populate some demagogic imaginary city based on an esoteric usage. So here was an analysis I debated, even if it acutely defined a topic as I made notes.

Analysis aside, marine life was a vise to make men agitate like zany canines in a fit of a ferality morale.

To tolerate my new abode's abuses, I became, besides a marine, some metafigure: somebody hired as one wily to notice how everybody here behaved. As a monitor, I became removed or as one remote, here yet in an isolated or even a safe zone. Nobody can abuse me, my solace raved, as I'm utopic in a topos of a topic of a loco locale.

To be sure, my basic abuse was over, in a far ago cadet arena, so now I more made to fit in as one man amid a fine few. It abated agony to copy how avid average men iterated a rote rot of a rotenone toxicity to relate how a marine's a hero. To do so, many delivered a tune named "A Marine: Him."

A Marine: Him

On a woman or a man alike
To defy morality
He paraded as a cad agog
In a penile revery
But a bufu tabu Xanadu
Cuba coke virility
Can amuse him in Uranus
As a sybarite marine.

But a majority rarely dove to so low a level. Even if a few abase marines abominated any morality in a parody to gag a polite citizen, an uniterated O.K. of amity tolerated abuse. Below abase levity was a serenity to let a marine caper, as a marine had a duty to go to war. As I resonated "A Marine: Him," I never awarely made "him" as one to be me, but I was aware how any war awoke federal ire to decimate, deracinate, damage, raze; to win over any rival. I had a hope my code duty to Colonel Ahi made me vital in a home base sinecure.

*

"Dave, get a data file for an arid ecology. We have got a notice to go live like cavemen in Iran. A Hamadan aga had a mite hole he lived in, aside some wadi. By solar image remote, he gave locales of enemy moves (or, in a mirage, moves of enemy locales) as images are wavy by caloric averages. An avocatory 'come' made him, on a dare, go home to his A. Minor abode, but as a caravan of an elite paramilitary body came to ride gun, a kamikaze hit. Aga Kane was eliminated, executed, as abusively were many more. Now it is upon us. A fire cures a fire cure," Colonel Ahi bowed.

"Aga Kane? Dare we deduce his oratory finale? *Rosebud*," I ran a peril of a rebuke, but a more dire peril arose to vex us.

A fire cures a sinecure. My fireside dates abated, I made do to go.

We were not in a legitimate war, as afar as Iran, Iraq, or any xenozone were to be defined as a war arena, but amity wore bare to make many defy my native mud. A marine had a core to be focused as a live wire to set a lure for an enemy hate.

But even if Iran as a verity were no zone for a definitive war, I was aware to be wary. We had a care to hide, for if an enemy saw us, a jihad era war of a type was a likely to-do to become some future for us. In a move to be careful, I separated a file nobody saw. I gave Colonel Ahi my databases of aridity, but as a ruse we behaved as if a game war in an arid ecology motivated us as a mobilized unit. One to five veteran aces of abuse by military severity came to give some benefit of a memory he had agony to relive. Colonel Ahi tolerated everybody so damaged, as a marine to have done duty was a case for a medical operative to pacify. Merely pacify? Cure was a rarity.

So we behaved as if on a regular utility run. A decode duty here, some note to put in a code to hide how it elucidated a vital item, a time for an Ahi literature seminar: average vapidity hid a new executive pose.

Some de Sade Marat of a medic inoculated us in a laboratory nobody came to, for it operated a serum utility for a malady panorama, toxic ozone gas abuse to nude mole rat ebola lice fever. Any rarely likely malady had a cure, we were humored, if one got inoculated in a laboratory before he degenerated in agony. To have some side pox or a fever as a rebate for a dose was a puny pity.

"But it elucidates an exotic obit, as a rare few ever awaken in a wake, done for in a fit of ebola lice fever."

At a future date to be named at a time gone by, we were to be removed. At a mid eve? Six A.M.? Anybody validated any rumor, as Ahi had opened every notice to be delivered afar. Ahi. Was it a likely ruse for Ahi to have made so buxom a bosom of a rumor up?

*

Amana came to me by notes a serenade delivered, as a hired ukulele diva duke gave me her alohas. Even as it evoked a love for emotive ceremony, my memory made Tiny Tim awaken one more time, to ravage tunes of ages ago. Her uke duke did it as a gag of a gig. As a pure sonata-like delivery related a bit of Amana's episodes, I revised every note to become some pixy disavowal of a purity to be reviled. Enamored of an ability to be raw, I came to berate her amity refined in a memory by some nemesis of a pop idol. Even if Amana had awarely no care to make me recapitulate Tiny Tim, I had a calamity to deter.

A tune, however it originated, emanated in a mated opus I revised in a heresy to debate her as I did imagine her episode to relate some simulated omen of Amana, in as afar as it opened a Mama/ Papa- recap of a tune.

Rev a Puny Reve to Me

Come baby to take me
Before cat-o-nine-tale mice wake me
Rededicate to make memory
Rev a puny reve to me

Some nap on a pipe toke
Revised in a revery to poke
Bikini babes of ape magazines
In a fit of amity.

But I'm in a hope for a sucu-
Bus of a come mute date
For as I'd awaken I've taken
A ride for a cute mate

Come baby give to me
How I can elope to be hoped in
A rider in erogeny zone
Rev a puny reve to me.

So he raved on, as I did, in a sidecar of a rotary bike
motored on a ses of a tina run on an enina gasoline. My
copy made his over, as Amana's imaginary vocabulary
became mine to take for a ride. To make more havoc,
I yet emanated a power of an evoker, as every bit of a
bone mot I bit on ate more to bite. Waves of a salivary
nature made vapor a very wet agility lane.

To Salivate to Saturate My Mate Marine

To salivate to saturate my mate marine
To bake some favorite rare fare delicacy
To wit: a licorice banana mojo bar
Of animated acolyte virility
But as I salivate to his anatomy
Desire has a duty to be done by me.

So many dive for abalone done by me
To tabulate repute can open a marine
Barometer of a gale core's anatomy
But every dame rates as a fine delicacy

To any man of average virility
So now I've got a job in a libido bar.

I ride my pole like firemen on a bare bar
In a recital of a love I've done by me
To savages agog apace to base virility
Betimes an enemy's anenome marine
Police come to refute my fine delicacy
By cover up of any bared anatomy.

But if a deputy's up on anatomy
He can imagine how a woman of a bar
Owes anyone to bare her ace delicacy
So to repel I give hope to be done by me
Like women agilely forebode to some marine
Her uterine hosana to virility.

To be a fugitive to vile virility
Takes up a paradoxical anatomy
Derived as an ecology by a marine
Base habitat is not a pure marina bar
As I let on if anybody done by me
Made hepatitis execute delicacy.

But I defy definitive delicacy
To ride some pole to motivate virility
So men arise to hope to ride to be by me
To be tutored a love by my anatomy.

Paraded as a lady major in a bar
I salivate to saturate my mate marine.

Marine bar anatomy virility delicacy done by me
Delicacy done by me marine virility bar anatomy
Bar anatomy delicacy virility done by me marine

Beloved inamorata vixen Amana made me pine for a date we'd unite to decide we were done, by me, by her. Us, as an avid unit of a copulative fix, elevated on an ebony cumulus of a foreboded ozone rip of a resonated ave for a zig of a zag of a laser. As a sayonara to me, her ukulele serenade gave notice to menace. How it evocatively fit a marine posed on a pike to be mobilized!

*

One mid-eve, we came to be rotated in a move to be gone. Were we doped? I sat upon a bare fuselage tatami mat in a jet, in a daze. Colonel Ahi beside me was awake betimes I woke, but in a likewise daze. Below, a watery body made wave miles enumerate time.

We had a tidy kit of operative devices in a camo decor of utility for a gamut of aridity zones. As a security delivery, were we to go below in an anemo dive? My bivy had a sac of a parabale. Not ever educated as an anemo diver, I was a bit agitated. In a core basic abuse regime for any marine, were we not in a line to be tutored as an anemo diver? I somehow eluded a vital item of a basic abuse regime.

"Colonel," I began in a timid ahem. "I do not, I was, um, unused in any capability to dive."

"Be sure to do how I do. Memorize cinematic agility. We have no huge dare to rise to. Somebody gives an 'up-at-'em,' a hole gapes, a rope takes us on a wire to fate, so parabales open upon exit. I do take care to do but one bit as a cinema hero. My line? Geronimo!"

Geronimo. So many cinema to cinerama dives in an anemocity zone were vocalized in an unaware homage to him, an American apex of a native power. I meditated in a desire to become so powered a native natural enemy, to dive for a cosine line to be set alit upon a safe mesa. My renegade hero led an unapologetic ave to nobody, but any to dive by parabale gave to him a salute by name. For a Minuteman or Icarine marine, "Geronimo" was a final oral ode to one's isolated elegy.

Later I became bored. An up in an ozone delivery time to some site made my life go pale. To be here, set in a fuselage, put on a voyage to no definite finale made me pine for a cone, some sonic eraser of a hazy hum. A hum, in a verity, did emanate to defer acutely resonated A notes, as a lute tunes on a tone to go forever. If I were beside my sanity, how Ahi managed in a likewise zone made me gaga. He was a man of icy serenity.

"Colonel Ahi, how is it—?"

A nod abated any more yap. I saw in a pixel of an age: *he* had ululated on an A-note tune tone. To make me mad? Enure me? We were not amused, as a royal adage had it.

"Up at 'em!" a mate gave notice we were to dive.

Below, I saw a solidity. No vegetative life, but a luna-lit ivory finery made Zone L a cozy locale for a marine base habitat.

I did as Ahi made me note to do. My parabale wire lined up on a rope to be led, I generated a fury to levitate by pure temerity. Colonel Ahi before me gave his itemized itinerary to some co-pilot. A pane wiper opened an exit agape for us, as a nice but avid aloha paw eked us on. In a cinema role to be some daredevil, I lowed a "Geronimo" (more cowed I was), as I hit an anemosity.

My parabale canopy did open. A yo-yo-like yaw eluded a fatality, but I yet agonized, aware to hit alit as agilely set as one can, in a somer-ine move to defuse body damage. To do so, my body made move to rapel, as a novice lined on a piton on a dive to go below amuses a Himalayan.

In one more jot, I caromed upon a pivot, as a comic in a cabaret apes an ape to fake some natural analogy to his animal ability. For a bit, I was O.K.

*

A ten A.M. of a time zone removed emanated in a digitized aside to dupe me. Here, time was on a pace before sun-up. A rare humidity made me decide we had alit in a negative zone: some site nobody was aware was in Iran. I, for one, was unaware we'd even alit in Iran. I, for one more care, saw I was alone.

We were "we" before we dove, but I never examined any parabale canopy beside me. Had Ahi dove to live, he'd of a surety be sure to notify me. But as of one date later, I came to rely minus on a "we" to be more set on an "I."

Colonel Ahi was AWOL or MI (to put an A here was a typical usage conovowel elides). Icy minutes in an isolated agony made me wary to figure how a marine can use his ability to live by wit alone. Many more minutes of a cumulative panic eliminated any hope to be saved. If anybody were here to save me, he hid. I became fixed on an image: nomad enemy men in a dune-hid operative pyramid of a remodeled utility base were wise to monitor a parabale diver in any case before salutes or alohas. I became, herefore, some caricature: man in a beret (unicap of a military forager or a rat of a marine) set on a savage rite to fit in an enemy locale.

Some rat? I solely hoped I had a rat ability to forage. However, as I roved over a mile to note my fix in an ecological oven, I became hot. A mid-A.M aridity rose, so here was I, set up in Iran. Or, Iraq? A military navigator in a jet on a parabale delivery had useful ability to divine so basic a federality line. But as a military nabob on a facile job as a forager, I was agog.

Any capability to do my duty to forage was academic. I had aced a seminar in Esoteric Animal Edibility, but in a live run, I was a loser.

As a loser, I wavered amazed in a maze daze to go very far in a locus of a hocus of a pocus. Every figure gave some similarity to mirages of itemized unanimity: mesa, taxicab, opal of abalone, deposit of ore, rice layered in anise cake, zareba dominated idol of a civilized aborigine race.

Vegetatively covered in acerose pikes, Idol Idaho (to cite how it evocatively modeled America's Idaho) rose to power as a god of a tiny top.

"Open, oh Idaho, sesame to deliver a bakery deposit of edibility." My sanity here was a dynamite keg. Any bit of a lit originality was a fuse to faze my debilitated ego.

"Come to me, my son, in a fidelity to be fed."

I'd imagined a monotone, vocalized in a fit of idol emanated amity. However evasively rare so barefaced a dare was, I decided it utile to do how it evoked, as if an average validity were rife to make some ceramic idol a live god. A famine was a valid abuse to defer, if at ever I had an ability to defer any famine. But, as I put a digit upon an acerose bit of a zareba wire-like cover, I had a zany time to devise how it opened.

"Is it open?" I renewed a bid.

"It is."

"Up at a top?" I saw a tiny bit of an open adit, above him. "I'm a marine, not a raven."

"One makes a fate to do."

To debate some god, as if a holy hero were human, elucidated a ruse to delude, but as an amulet acolyte cadet, I had an evocative debility. To be deluded in awe was a care for anybody so tutored.

A vegetative razory wire covered every side but above. To be fed, I deliberated a lacerated agony v. a sated edacity. But, aha! Some mole type nose poked up as a radar of above-level ecology. He was a wary waverer, acute to bury his animality below as I was above, but I here saw a mole mode to copy. Dig it! I dug.

In a bit of a time, my hole led in, in a zone by my vocal idol. In a mute nod of a delivery, he gave me benefit of a pit of a pot of edibility. Baba ganuge, humus, ale-like kefir, a waxy papered olive pita, kid. I had at it, ate to my sated avarice to dine before my body retired in a coma degenerative haze.

*

Some time later, I woke to be beset in a din, as a holy furor of idolizer Ali Babas ululated. Amid a razory vine cover, I made no move to be met. One before more came to give token amity to God Idol Idaho. Delivered edibility bites of a native fare were rife, so my refuge became some taco wagon of a falafelite depository.

Faces agog in a devoted awe raved a demonic elegy for analytical exegesis. I was amused. I was, I decided, in a locale to be set up as a muse. More yet, I was a vice-banana to some god. An evocative vocality can ahem a finer amity to be donated, betokened as enumeratively more bites. As an evoker, I'd emit a desire to give more by some faked iterated idol oratory. My monotone god Idaho made his evocative bid: "I desire more."

Were my power isotopes on a diminutive level? I focused on an evoked, "I desire more," but I made nobody cede to give more. For a more focused evocative fix, I figured a vocality was a dare to do. Besides, if I vocalized "I desire more," my vocalized evocative desire'd abet a magic intoned awe to somebody non-American, as an Americanized ave had a purely sonic opacity to some nomad isolated in an afar arid ecology.

So, my tones of oratory focused, "I desire more."

My god! A majority came to bow, in a renewed ululated avidity. Venerated as an idol, I was in an idol idyl, in a nexus of exuberated amity. My natives of a rave were dopes, or of a rare humility to be so taken, in a haze by some fake god. As a god, I had a duty to bedevil everybody, to make men agog in awe for a power of a nature so super, it emulated atomic eliminator ability. To do so, did I have to decimate some race, deracinate some colony, set up a famine, sever a lake, have water imitate wine, make some cadaver arise to come to life? My god ability was uneducated. I desired a holy façade, to bare more fury to make more love me. Me, God Idaho, God Idol of Iran.

"I desire more," my rage rose to ravage my mice men as I, for a giver of a love to be, fired an ire to be doted upon. I was a god agog in a fog of a ruse rosary misery. My fury had a rare dynamic ability to motivate.

More did atone to come, to give more to be my loyal adulative degenerates in a love for a power of one super in a supine pose, for I retired abase to be hid as a new epidemic of avid emotive generosity came to my den.

It, or a lot of it, aped an aboriginal animality: moved! It agitated a wavy viper agility. Viper as in, uh oh. A rare taxonomy viper elite set up a hexagon of animosity to monitor anybody so delicately human as one to be here. To be put in a viper abode was a fate no god as I was ere had.

I made some move to go to my hole, but a viper of a more mobile homebody nature had agilely moved in. As a god or idol or even a comic of a vice-banana to some god, I was a dud. If I let on I was in a fix, as a non-idol of any type god or, as a mere man, I'd abuse my nomad amenity base. No god is one to beg. I had a negative lot of ability to save my bacon, in any case. My renovated abode was a lively pit of a menace to be rid of a.s.a.p. I saw a solitary den exit: up.

Above, by my idol Idaho's apex, an open adit emulated a domicile gate to liberate me. But if I were to go to get atop Idaho, my cover as an idol elucidator of a holy vice-banana'd abate. Were my rubes of a fine robe humility so set in a rut of a holy furor as, on average, to be mad if a man imitated a god in ruse role? Below, a vipery gape came to bare maw in an acerose severity.

Some vines of a lace nature gave me leverage to get on up, as Idaho had a few inutile pores of enured anatomy for anybody but an ape to use. My marine basic abuse memory had a similar onus of a rope/ piton exam of a human/ ape/ bug elevator ability, but on it I had aped an ape lamely. Now I was on it anew, in a zone to go however I had agility to go. Many minutes of agony later, I came to my top, above menaces of animal animosity, vegetative tenacity, my limited ability to rise to fix a fix I got in, or any fury to be had, as a marine set amid enemy rubes.

Upon an apex above wadi mesas, I saw I was amid a wide horizon. Average miles of a wan Iran opened as I rotated, in a gyre to deliberate how I'd imagine my safety to be secured. A lone caretaker of ewes abided in a bucolic utility role not afar. A likewise solitary lad ate dates upon a palomino camel of a pony located in a zone hereby. My many natives of idol awe were gone, so to vary my gig, I waved as I cajoled in ironic inanity.

Below, a nomad I did omit in a gaze to notice as I'd examined afar educed an ave. He had a gun, as everybody did in a zone viper animosity populated. Everybody but a marine delivered by jet on a parabale run. As he was an Irani, my vocality was inutile. To be vocal, I was a Tower of a Babel asininity, but I used a mime set of animated agility to beg, elucidate, refer, et.

al. Awarely, he got it. In a jif, a rope rose to dip above me, set as a life line by some device to be lowered as a lever as it operated on a base set in iron.

I rose to be saved.

*

"Abu jab," or a likewise bit of an Arabic-imitative line woke me.

Had I taken a sedative? Surely yes, a serum of a verity nature came to be given in a dose to me, to make me bare my motives. A meditative power or ability was of a sedative nature, but I had a set apology: to be tired if anybody came to berate me. Was I here politely? My tag of a dog ID eluded a name to give my job a legitimacy. My beret, arid ecology camo, pin a marine wore to secure toxicity's exit in a hari-kari dose? Every note toned a military tune to my serenade. To be here, put in or on an Irani site, set up a recon avidity. Mode by mode, my pose posed a ruse no mere visitor used on an average voyage.

But as if I were put on a legitimate parole, no volatile, rude, demonic, or asinine delegates of an enemy made my visit an agony, yet. I was on a semi-liberated, open itinerary to go zone to zone; but, in an abode dug as a hole for a mole, no zone was a cozy home, nor a base for operative havoc. It, on average, was a bore. My parade to case more was a duty like some coyote had as it awarely cased a cave for a bat. I bet a coyote never ate bat.

As I bore boredom, I figured I had it O.K.: e.g., a Mayan-era marine taken as an enemy by Toniná savages in a military role had a vile time before demise came to defer agony. Nobody made me define my role viz-a-viz any gig as a god agog in a move to be fed. If I was a con or a fake, did anybody care?

Some hypo came for a fix one more time. Fine. So my role to take verity serum in a dose-by-dose case was on a sure ride to define me by my marine basis as one to be demobilized. In average basic abuse, we were made wise to how an enemy doc op. operated. One cure, we'd alit upon, arose to some rare few. A few erotica sages of avidity to deter, arose to defy serum of a verity by powered ability to reset a fix a hypo fix elicited. I recovered a memory how a marine, by focus on one sideline, had a mode to limit any damage. To limit or evade damage, he'd imagine love. By love, we focused on a nexus of Eros.

A syrum of a verity, however, in a dosed-over erotica-remade focus of avidity, posed a dare. We were given a note to beware how a mix of a hypo fix, aside so fixed a focus as one to have sex as a POW in an enemy hole made for a loco fit, educed a zany fun amok an edit of a marine him.

I revived an image to recap Amana by memory, to revive more loves. Is it a rabid inanity for anybody to be loco for every dame? Duty made me do my duty, but any duty had a duty to remit a finely done fine to remunerate more for amore.

More verity dose waves of a loco caloric avidity made me rise to be some hedonic avatar in a new id idyl. I came to be set in a rave hereby to be desired, as a sexy fix. A desire for a fix evocatively made me remove my lower unit of a regular uni camo to be bare for anybody. Any comer, on a top or a pose below in erotic utility was a fare game hen of an ovulater in every pot of a rut.

"I am Eros," I vocalized, "I come for anybody."

Motivated as a man, akin a penile simulator, I made my daze general as I roved in a demi-naked erogeny parade.

"Come here, my human Eros," an Irani delivered a line set in an Americanized avocatory lexicon. "A lady desires a love mate."

My lady was in a cabana—not a mule hut. A denizen of erotica led, as my lower id unit iterated a rise to power.

"Ali loxen," a line gave notice to some piper.

A melody began. A libido waxed. An adit opened. I saw, in a repose to have me, my lady, naked at one pit of an erogeny zone.

To be sure, my duty made for a tug of a sexy fit, as a lube gave her an avidity to be fixed. I did, in a marinely love. Semen I per a fi-fo-fum, I was a titan in a pud on a make to be her anal analyzer.

Anal? As an analyzer, I figured it opened as an anal orifice. My ability to figure holes of a sexy nature was a habit a marine has. If a lady desired an anal amore fix, I was in it! In a dutiful avidity, my copulative virility generated a jet I delivered as a man in a fit of a duty done to be lured in a luridity my lady made.

Her oh-oh-oh in an ah-ah-ah abated. As a finale, her body rotated in a rococo kimono nobility to bow. In a kimono to bow? Oh oh.

I removed a cover of Arabic arabu to be face to face.

"Colonel Ahi!"

How I'd abased a duty to be done!

*

We were to be litigated on a sodomy rap, as Irani law executed any sodomites. A solicitor elucidated a capital itinerary for eradicability devices, as if a menu were to decide fate for us.

"Acetylene fire, mirage deluge water, a rope for a tug-o-war on a body to be severely severed, a bite by viper, a cup of a toxic elixir, acid acetone for a Noxema cure, bury-me-not-in-a-hole litany degeneracy for a daze to be lived as a verity to have for a demise, lacerated abuse cut in a diced agony, decapitated as a capon in an ISIS opera for a few amused elites."

"It is a game," Colonel Ahi rated any move to cower us.

"I beg an ahem. It is a fate to be done," Solicitor Orema had a duty to demur.

"I was in a dope daze, revised in a feminine get-up, as a woman in a harem. I woke to be raped. I made no move to sodomize," Colonel Ahi gave his avowal in a fine fury, gaze fixed upon Orema.

"My vices are rife, but I have no desire to sodomize, rape, have sex upon or in a man," I deposed. "I was unaware my fake wife was a man."

I was one to hope to hide my military nexus as an amulet acolyte to Colonel Ahi. He now evoked a delicate role, not as a marine but as a native luminary, somebody to be taken as an iterater of exegeses. Emulate him, I saw I had a wise duty to do. Besides, I was an evoker of a power.

"In a legal ecumenical arena, we have no veracity to rebut. Every law is a given. Every rule comes as a holy canon, if I can analogize to Vatican usages a pope devises in a rosary to deliver a law above natural or average legality," Solicitor Orema had an academic ability to regulate holy vapor in a conovowel usage to put on a solid amen of an amenity.

So we were solely to solicit Orema to set up an executed utility. Some men of a hero malady were loco for an agony to deliver a definitive demise. Many more desired every celerity to be done to get it over.

"Are we solely given a menu here for every fate?" Colonel Ahi solicited a new exile. "Can I have some fate not on it?"

"Ah," Orema was in a role to make do. Colonel Ahi gave some notice he was agile to be delivered an executed elegy. "We can apologize to defer in an edit of a type to redo menu files. If it amuses a jury, juridicature maven, or an elite, debate can evade set itinerary damages."

"I beg a par of a done coda," Colonel Ahi began an oratory for Orema to recapitulate for any juridical exegesis. "A coma can edify medical originality by rigid isodynamic ages if a man is iced in a cube for a future to be later. I vow a desire to benefit, abet, or open Irani medical ability to sedate to put us on ice cubes as in a refer. In a refer of an ice box, I bet I can, in a vegetative reve, be put alive for a date far in a future to be taken as one can arise, waken, or un-ice his amoral abuses in a new Irani morality, to be saved."

Orema was amused at any rate to move to favor an inane model of evasive mobility. To be put on ice was, anybody saw, a sure homicide device to demobilize some de Sade sac of a hari-kari-loco wagerer.

"Isis ice," Colonel Ahi denoted a Nile pyramid avidity (not a new ISIS exodus) as one to be revived in a future life.

"Duty to be done," my marine salute-like vocality made Solicitor Orema get it.

In a nod, Orema made his exit. A putative date was alit upon. Orema had an alibi, made some case, did a jig. I never examined it, as every ceremony hid in a legality we were removed afar of, as if in a locale nobody visited, even on a dare. Were we done par a par of a done? Paroled on a bet of a futile future?

Some time later, in a few icy minutes, an arid ozone came to beset us, in a fume to come done.

*

My visage wavered as I woke to waves upon a titanic, or at any rate, some huge navy caravel on a voyage to my future home. Beside me, Colonel Ahi was awake, so we wavered in unison as a medic elucidated a tale to get us up on episodes of a time we were rigid in a coma. Not even a decade had aged us in ice before we were taken. A naval or a marine based unit on a recon of an Iran enemy line located us.

"Iran is an enemy yet?" I figured Iran as an enemy far ago. Not even a valid enemy, but one for useful abuse.

"Forever, it evokes, on an average to be done never. Iran is an enemy we have."

"How are pirates of a renegade federality policed, if an enemy takes up an ire to do more?"

"Pirates?"

I had a memory to revisit, of a pirate renegade federality . . . Somali? Bali? Xanadu? Some Sahara zone gave a pirate pod a haven as a favor on a rebate basis. If it operatively became some duty to regulate so colonized a menace, piracy duty was a lemonade run. A lone liner in a façade to be docile hid a marine core caravan of a firepower ability to rebuke. Tales of awesome rebuke were regular, as an average pirate was of a temerity nature, very likely to take some dare (not awarely beware) to beset any luxury liner.

"Oh, I get it. I can elucidate how it, as a final utility, came to be decided. A definite benefit opened as a pirate colony was a military pod. It abided as any marine based unit, in a cameradic agility to be fit as an enemy menace. We merely hired every pirate colony for a tidy sum, as a duly deputized enemy to hit anybody we named as an enemy."

"Pirates are now America's enemy's enemy?"

My deducer ability revived.

"America?" he hesitated.

As I focused, I saw an atypical unitunic of a paramilitary color in a mode to define futurity. He wore robes of a new unit, of a federality my time, per a hap of ado, never educed.

"U.S.A."

He faked an unaware tic of a gape to deny my veracity. Many medical executives of an ago yore had, as a joke, faked an inability to get a basic usage my conovocality made, but I figured it as an exam a medic executed as a ruse to verify my sanity. Comatose for a time, we were to be put upon in enumerative types of exam. A laboratory dynamic of a ferocity to be wise made men use deliberate ruses as a leverage to get a rat in a maze to behave.

"Hum. U.S.A. was a power of eras ago. Now it is isolated. It abated every war it ever abusively began. Or, it, as a federality, merely capitulated as a war agitator, in a move to reposit an economy gone to pot."

"If it as a power is a bygone, how are we here now?"

"A new unity hegemony had originated a police forager unit, in a move to take more taxes, as it evasively were. By tirade name, Mobility Limited, a polyfaceted utility federated in a fidelity to monetary bases, operates as a developer of exotic economic edifices."

"Is it, or, are we non-alined in any fidelity to some federality?"

"Yes. In a line, we fare solely by wages of a savage rapacity. Now, I have related a bit of an exegesis. Anybody to wake many dates in a future takes a time to get it."

"Are many, were many before us iced in a coma to wake later?"

"A few. It is a laboratory game. But, I dare figure, nobody (yet even any) to be put on ice has in a totality come to recover ability to be how a man is, in *every* fit usage, to be."

*

So my federality, let alone my fidelity (to my wife to be, Mimical Ecole Parole, marine base), was of an era gone by. Solely Colonel Ahi was a nexus alive to bygone times.

"I hesitate to ratify his American elegy," Colonel Ahi debated, in a tone to be wise to be wary.

Were we not in a fate to defer unawarely to however a future came to be defined? Any tale related in a recovery zone for aged-in-ice men of ages ago was a tale likely to be colored in a ruse for a sage to later iterate to his amused amigos as a game he devised. Aware how a military humor emulates a levity to make dupes of anybody taken in, I had a tenacity to tolerate some fib of awesome size. To be taken in on average, my tale here has a fabulosity to be debated, as anybody can aver a relater of a likely tale can edit as one to fib in one-sided agility.

My before set-upon academic onus, as one to pen a paper, evoked a bipolar avowal. On one pole, my paper abated, as every tutor I'd used in an academy role was a goner. On one more pole, my paper abided, as a paper of a tome can abide, to become some deposed exegesis of a time some life lived. As one relater of a tome, in a finale, had it, "Can I go? No. But on I go."

To go to my tale, herefore, some finales of erudite tomes evocatively nominated a few exit alohas I'd emulate.

"So we row on, in a kayak at a gale, refuted every time to times ago."

" . . . he was in a fury like mad as I raved a yes I do Yes."

"Are we not in a finery to cogitate so?"

"Surely we come to more avidity to aver, 'Amen, even as I come, Jesus!'"

"In every zone he was a native, for everybody had iterated a tale to recapitulate him."

"I'm agog as I've come home."

"He let a gaze set upon a fine caravel on a horizon afar."

"One javelined a cadaver of a dog at 'im, in a ravine."

"Mañana's one more date."

"He was anon a goner on a wave to wave, gone forever in an ebony dim, afar."

"Over a river a laser of a sun of a fire came to divide some deluge set of a cumulus omen of awe."

" . . . to meditate how anybody can imagine serenity for any body to be put in a hole to be here."

"Surely no to-do for an oral-oral ave. Beloved."

"At a finale, here were no finales."

" . . . as it is a sole life forever aside by side we have, my Lolita."

"Now, everybody—"

But any finale was a foregone parapet of an edifice yet in a tale to be figured. I more had a desire to devise how I'd agilely navigate now.

"Are we recovered?" I sat up, aware to be deliberate.

Colonel Ahi likewise made moves of a karate delicacy, to define how every fiber of atony was of an atony to tune to tone.

"We can elevate deliberately but at a pace to make sure we have managed a natural agility, but as one so focuses, one loses a natural ability to do. For a natural ability never (or in a very rare case) has a duty to make sure to manage nature."

To mete so typical an analysis, Ahi gave notice he was O.K.

*

A minute before we were to be led on an open aloha policy to visit everybody, some siren evoked a general alarum.

"A game war," Ahi relegated it, in an abusive tone.

To him, a simulated élan enameled every move here. Men exuberated in a fake pep of avidity to bare savage desires. Everybody ran in a metered isodynamic unanimity to parody some regimen a moron of unaged ability'd imagine, to facilitate some diminutive mobilized utility by tiny token enemy men in a game-size model of a military rage. Busy solely to be busy, not in a move to do but in a move to make do, was Ahi's analysis. Or, it emulated a re-do, to be redone many times in a revised edit of a bad original.

As a veteran of operative ferocity, he had a habit of a marine to time mariner agility.

"Tic a toc," Ahi began an iterated oral unit of a bit of one minute to ridicule how a below average mariner operated, as if agog on a rum oral exam. "It is a benefit of irony no vital enemy's upon us."

An Uzi fired. A volatile magazine delivered a deluxe-caliber animosity to defy some rival anonymity.

"Dynamite demagogy," Colonel Ahi berated every ratatat as a firepower abuse.

But in a minute more, lines above came to lower a dory. Five men of a rude façade rode to row, as one rode gun, as if in a pose to betoken a Delaware River episode many decades ago. Waves on a helical axis emanated in a volume to rotate P.O.V., as it opened a new acute gap of a gape for us. A bow of an enemy became some luxury liner.

"Aha, now it is a validity," Colonel Ahi joked in a humility to defy his analysis. "I have to revise. My pate yet is unawares, in ice. My camera power of ocular acumen is in an agitative focus of inutility. Relate to me how it emanates in every move to wage damage."

"Some ebony rag of a pale figure's atop a dory pole, put up a-bow. A figure makes an ex of ivory below a famine mug," I defined, as Ahi made time to recuperate."

"Bones in an ex of a femora below a bony face?" he posed an iconic image.

"Yes!"

As I gazed on, Ahi related in every move how I saw it emanate. By ropes, agile men alit upon a level of a mesa-like level. Uzis on a safety to menace, some few operated as usurer elites in a capitalized economy, to vow everybody here had a haven as any citizen of a regular economy has, as a bag opened agape for any jewel or a total of any lira, peso, yen, et. al. In every case, nobody rebuked. It emulated a polite rite, for a pirate revery to forage for a sum of a pile to take. By gun amen or as a rebate type tax of a wise regularity, many luxury voyager agas awarely gave to be safe.

"So, nowadate we fit in a piracy regime," Colonel Ahi resolutely posited.

"Are we no more yet in a marine regime, to be separated as ice cubes un-iced in a future we have no capacity for?"

"In a Japanese vocal usage, we have 'mu' to vocalize to put a line to some not-a-negative-nor-a-positive-to-be-decided ahem. I'd aver a mere mu."

*

We had an anomaly to decide: how it, a future life here, came to be related as a ruse by some pirate. No tale, however elucidated in any veracity, had a duty to be but a ruse. Pirate code ruled.

One more bit of an anomaly came to me: we were yet in a conovowel ecology. Here, futures afar, an a/b/a/b/a lexicon operated as in a heretofore time. Per a hap of a fate, we woke not awake, but in a comatose daze, like some reve. Hereby, we were yet in an iced Eden or a Hades or in a mid of a level itinerary, to be separated evasively forever in a fix of a mobility maze. To be mobilized as a marine was a minor abuse, given a lifetime fixed in a mobility maze.

So many dates I had executed every bit of use by conovowel usage, my natal usage was a vocality gone to disuse. Had it, as a vocality to generate my basic epic, ever orated in any capacity for a model of a me before now? A tenet of a type posited a hypotenuse line to fix A to B in a logical aha to make men awed: as one vocalizes or uses a set usage to cogitate for a final awake time, so set is one's usage forever, in a Paradise, Hades, or any likewise zone to take him over as a nonalive liver of a sometime life now arisen or abased in a wavery vapor of a demise.

Were we not alive? To cogitate was a basis of a live human, or an ability to live by. But as I more cogitated on usages, ability, humanity, marine life, pirates, et. al., I became more remote, removed in a recovery to be beside my body. Beside my body, my cogitated ego sum arose to make me decide we were yet alive. To so decide was one more level a live human operates on, in an average life.

Many japes alit upon a fire to vex us, as if every ruse to rebut any recovery we were to have were set on a deliberate pace to defer. As a limit of a cal of a culus is on an axis of one x/y line forever on a lane to but abut, I came to verify how I was in a fate to never awaken in a totality to be liberated.

Anon, a medical operative had a hypo to deliver a sedative to "cure" my cares.

"A cure? How?"

"It is a soporific. It abates every sore by benefit of a lazy daze haze," he mewed in a pure pule.

"But I've had a decade to be sedated as a cadaver. I desire some pep. A get up agitative fix of a hypo!"

"Relax. It is a more docile serenity to be set in a lazy haze, put in as one takes a nap in a fine finite repose," he resumed a tone to be like some guru, to make me do however I'd operate to cede to do.

Colonel Ahi gave him a body divot of a legitimate leg adit as one zone for a hypo to deliver a dose, but Ahi had a hide to hide below a sedative. His anatomy hide hid as a camo color evasively hid an animal in a habitat of a similarity zone, so medical operatives on a hypo delivery duty rarely had an ability to dig up any locale for a hit.

"A salami has a vanity nobody dare adore," he bared a salami-like hide to give his agile leg an atony to defy doses inoculated as a cure to pacify.

His agile medicine menace had a go repetitively before he put a cap on it.

As a bonus, I was agitated in a fever; it emulated a dose to me. My tired, unawakened, isolated inability to be me was abated in a fit of a negative rub.

"A cure can awaken a nature," my medic analyzed, exuded a tap of a code so some janitor opened a gate for exit.

"I bet it is open," Ahi saw, as it evoked a maze to be begun.

*

A pirate-made maze was one to bedevil a voyager. As I was in an awakened ire, my capacity for agile mobility was agitated. I had a hope Colonel Ahi had a surely deliberated avidity to navigate so demonic a lane, but I saw Ahi waver one more time. We were yet agog in a haze to be debile.

To navigate here, my caravel ago lore was an imagined erudite logic of a xebec origin. As a xebec of a time before my time by far abided in a cove for a safe coverage, some caravel of a more date-to-now era sat in a navy base basin. Upon an open utility run, a caravel of a xebec elevated on a wave ride to defy to be defined as a man-o-war. On a man-o-war, a mariner arose to do duty to ravage, so piracy was of a moral utility. To be fit in utile vanity, pirates alike had, over ages, a hope for a dynamic executive power apace some gig of a ruse to hide below a refined if average façade.

Cabin ecology here was as in a sub, as a limited use capacity decided any facile mobility was a no go. Puny moves agilely made do, so we were put in a can as a delicacy boned in a lube dew an avocado'd emanate, given a refinery for a fix. In a line we filed, eked as a tiny hose piped a watery pit-a-pat in a molecule H-O-H. A dim eke for any lit imagery managed a barely bared agape visibility. Before me, Colonel Ahi made gelatin edify to set, at a pace to come to now. Erase hopes of any celerity, he did aver in a mime demo to be some model of a deliberate mole.

Moles are/ were how a marine put as one to be hid in an enemy zone came to be labeled, as in a bygone life we had abided in, in Iran. "Are pirates an enemy for us as it is?" I resonated in a repetitive Bolero type tune to revisit an itinerary we never abated. As a mole was, I was or I yet am, in ever a dim abode.

Colonel Ahi levered a cabin open. A hole lit up a bit of it, as a wary visibility made some cages of a ménage come to life, for a habitat of a human animal arena. Here were some women exogamy venerated, a fop of a man in a cape to betoken a deluxe résumé. Some pirate mate, wily to deny his ability to dominate so baleful a habitat as one here, came to define his eligibility to be honorary caregiver of everybody, to refer in asinine humility to some laborer in a home for anile care.

"How are my fine women of a copacetic exile, my hale man of operatic amity?" he bade some general ave to be met.

In unison, everybody towed a cow of a cow of a tow, in an amicus of a hokum, as if in a vicarage-leveraged ozone. Beside so hazed a pat unity, we were sanity modeled in a levity for everybody to mimic.

"I'm in awe to be so met," Ahi bowed.

I, likewise, did a bit of a bow, in a gyre to some déjà vu move. Cinematic esoterica mixed in amid a holy ceremony canon. One memory renovated an image: viper agility manipulated as if a viper animality gave holy venom in a bite for a rabid ability to be saved. I mimed a vipery manipulative holy man.

It animated a locomotive levity. Loco motives, as afar as I divined in an evocative recovery, were vivid as azure doves in a cerise canopy. Here resonated a general inane havoc of a vocal abuse. My disability to get it awarely was atypical. A Babel of oral agility made me focus on every sonic unit. It opened a pit of a logical acute debate to defy my cinema hope to be set up in a set amid a conovocality colony. How any many camera tales of average yore made do by pat usages of a vocabulary to cover everybody, so none were set aside by limited ability to take note!

But as everybody beside me raved on, I saw it emulated a lifelike regularity. Conovocal usage was a rare model of oral utility. More typical, I came to face, was a humanity set agape by disability to figure how anybody new or exotic operated in a vocabulary no native here vocalized. As every "here" was afar in a relativity to separate "here" locales, I solely had a care to note how anybody ever educed a topic any separate locality posed.

In a move to secure similitude to ratify human

amity, we had a dare to take, to let everybody become liberated (as afar as anybody put on a xebec of a caravel of a renegade pod is ever in a liberated idyl). I made a deliberate move to set open every cage, to repel any pirate rebuke. Nemesis or amigo, he made no move to cavil as one gate gaped open in a domino dive model of a more-to-come nature. He merely retired.

One by more, my delivered amigos emanated in a move to be rid of a caged ecology. We were herefore mutely to pilot a caravan of agitated exiles on a voyage by caravel in a maze we figured as an agony for anybody to have to navigate, devised as a levity to but amuse bored apes. As afar as it amused an imagined anonymity, we were safe.

But anybody not amid us in a dim unanimity had use for an i-red ability to make so jet-ebon a refuge come to visibility. No holes of any camera size facility gaped open in a likely monitor ocular. I'd of a wager on iron ore pyrite have bet an ore lode we were monitored.

*

I'd imagined a time gap as everybody became soporific. One by seven (as Ahi, five cage mates, I, in a totality were) sat up in unison awake. How, as one, did everybody come to? Some titanic as in a Titanic abuse resonated. As a marine veteran, I deduced it as a din of a detonated origin. In a bit, an odor of a fire came to forebode demise by toxic oxygen, as every caravel edifice rib agitated in a semi-human agony. We were beveled on a dive to go below every wave.

"—'pedo hit," Ahi divined, as a veteran of a similar acumen.

Above, biped executives operated in a none-for-anybody panic. A remote panic of a pirate nature somehow amused us, as every man above made do for a security none hoped in any verity for anybody beside him.

Amused as I was, I was aware we had a finely tuned age limit of a time to go before we were late. Water emanated up in a rapidity to saturate, hip-elevated. Everybody moved in one rebel exit. I wagered if any pirate were to mug us in a fit of a finale, we'd eliminate him as a tiny mote by puny leverage.

Before we met any toxic acid, emanated as a fire made fumes, or any more water, as it arose, we came to some new, acerose rim of a hole, cut in iron. It was as if, in a detonated exit of acutely capitulated irony, fatality fate saved us. In a move to vacate, we solely had a go to get above by some lane made by dynamite damage. Bit of a bit, everybody got a cut or a sore, but any mere cut eked a relatively minor agony. Before we were done for, a tube developed as a pipe for a watery race. We were fired, as on a line by gun or as a silo fires a Minuteman on a parabola to zone zero.

For a volatile time, we were hot on a vapor of anemonic élan over every wave, like super elites of a volitative power. It abated. In a sayonara to levitated-above levity, we came to water, alit amid a refuse bonus. As a bonus, a set of overage refuse was a literal utile lifesaver, as an average wave put an item on a bob above water. A ligature tenacity made to fix a catamaran of every separate refuse bit as it alone came to be set aside by calamity.

No pirate had a likewise secured exit, as afar as I saw. An oh-oh of a wary type came to my ken. Erasure policy had, in a fare war ago, let a marine sub execute men on a maritime delivery run or of an enemy navy by gun if any were to be yet alive. But a more severe homicide hovered. In a jot of an elucidated edit, I saw a fin of a tiger or a mako cut a wake rudely red as a body bit of a leg in a bite relic imitated a senator of elated avarice rabid in awe to manipulate by lip a semi-gone cigar. Upon a catamaran, at any rate, demises of a jawed agony were not a fate yet in a future for us.

*

In a move to make time go, we deliberated over a gamut of inane games. Ahi repetitively tutored everybody, to make xenovocality more local. In as afar as everybody here was in a same locale, we had a care to relate to somebody so hereby zoned.

"I wave to some wave," he waved at a wave. "Waves are water. Overabove, waves are made by water, or, in it."

"A wave. Watery waves are water," an oral opacity came face to face. Bored in a pupil agog arena, tabula rasa docility was a face to hide fury.

"We move to water on a wave. Below, up," Ahi manipulated a salute to wave mobility.

"We move water. Are we waves?" One pupil, of a name like Linolena (her original I.D. of a name to go by was of a vocality Colonel Ahi made no move to copy) gave him a ride.

"Water," Ahi hit it in a demo to make Linolena wet. "Are we wet?"

"Are we we?"

"We're some. To be some, we're not an I, for an I's a solitary bit of a we. Some men are wet as a woman. Are we wet as a woman in a wave?"

"Wet are we? Women are wet?"

"I'm a man," Ahi lowered a gaze to his unit of average male virility. "Ye be woman. A man is one. So's a woman. One by more for a sum of a some comes as a we."

Did academy regimes of a Japanese rigor evoke some rite to berate?

"Some man is one dim item of a sum, as a woman is one to be some women of a sum."

A general inability to deliver a definitive tenor of use by rime for a pupil abated any more wise fakery by Colonel Ahi, but I had a tale by parody to relate, memorized as a model of a K-one level educator: A Tale for a Bob or a Jane.

To begin: "Examine Jane run. One Jane made some run. Examine how a Bob or a Jane ran. Examine Jane so Jane can examine Bob as a lad on a run. Examine Pogo run. Examine Pogo run as a dog. Examine Bob as a dog of a lad. Examine Bob examine Jane. 'Jane, can I get a leg up?' Examine how a Jane made a dog of a name Pogo bite Bob. One Pogo bit one Bob on a leg. A leg as in one sole leg up? Examine Bob as a biped. As a biped, a Bob is a lad of one leg, one more leg. Examine Bob examine Jane some more. 'Pogo, bite Bob one more time!' Jane has a care to run. Examine Jane. Jane cares. Examine Jane care more for a dog. As a dog, a dog of a name Pogo gives a lad of a name Bob a care to be nice. Bob, be nice. Give Pogo some bone, Jane. Nice Pogo."

My related epic of a rote tale parody made my mob amused in a vocabulary gone to Babel. Even a ludic unit as evocatively bun-in-an-oven as a male leg operated as a tune note, sonic in a purity to set a meditative tone for everybody to put aside.

So for a time we rode waves on anemo-dynamic emanated episodes. Adage validity seditatively made for a monotony Monopoly game dope-tokened amenity gave. More vital average desires of a potability water, of edibility fare were put on a remote level. Even as I was aware we were mobile to be gone to some locale to revive hope, mobility here had an "as if" itinerary. To be set in an anemo-dynamic ecology was evocatively to be put in a core focus of a gale. However it agitated a fury, we voyaged unaware.

Before famine came to make revery capitulate to misery, Fop Eli had a resolute model of a vile vitality to nominate. He'd, as a man of a care for everybody, let anybody have his amatory wine to sip to revive her (or, if a he be so led in a homo desire, his) avidity. His elixir of amatory generosity, seminal in origin, evoked an amity to put aside timidity, he did aver. As everybody was agog, every bit of Eli's inane bid evoked a sober avarice to be meditated upon.

Ahi, to disabuse repute we'd on average have had of a fine man, evoked a similar id of a bid.

"I can emulate raw ahi tuna, for a delicate lip."

As one more to be fare to give so some to be fed, I had a duty to give mine for a likewise solidarity. Solid as I was, I was aware how a vocal aloha had a basic inability to have some get it. As I was ever as of ago, tutored as an amulet acolyte, my capability to be set in an evocative jag operated as one to rile.

Before more bid more, my bid evoked an ahem of a female nexus.

"Oh."

"Oh Oh."

"Oh, a ho, huh?"

"Oh, I'd, uh uh."

As I evoked an unelucidated anatomy nod on a telewire-like delivery, Fop Eli made his operative cod unit adit open as if in a demo to make sure nobody was unaware how avid a fop of a man as Eli was, in every care to give some maw a sip. Even if a "no dice" veto had evaded every bid, a polite male had a desire to care for any female/ male maw.

*

In a very debilitated atony, we came to some solid ecology. Nobody had a map. I was even unaware to put us in any watery body by name, let alone some hemi/ demi/ semi zone. Was it a bit of a lot, as a dot of a Galapagos is amid a wide Pacific, or a tip of a lot of a locale to go many miles in or up or over, as an American imaginary forever is a reve for utopic averages of an unexamined analogy? To put us in an analogy, we were more like Galapagos aborigines, isolated on a dot, esoteric as a reve can imagine. My hope for an American exodus (or is it a hope to go home to America?) was a remote, demoralized elegy.

But at any rate, my life here made for a cozy degeneracy. Colonel Ahi was of a loyal amity. Fop Eli was a wit of a rake. Linolena had a 'tude to refuse hokum, as every female here had. Uma was an apex of isodynamic if one-sided agility, to go by her ability to debate solid exegeses in a vocality nobody got. Ida lit a fire by fuse to defile decorum or abominate boredom. Erika made faces of epidemic ironic erogeny to repel any non-Amazon avarice to cop a sexy doxy. We had a fine line dynamic of a city-like site to be civil, as everybody here was in a revival unit.

One case to define was, as I duly did a duty to relate, how alone we were. Put on a dot in a Pacific or on a lot of an America-sized abode, were we located in an isolated or a merely remote zone? Nobody was in a hereby vicinity, but I hesitated as I came to decide we were some solo colony. Relic ivory came to verify some civilized abode had abided at one time here. Jewel icon ivory, made to facilitate some rite to dine by luna was one tenet I posed of a sup analysis. As an item a diner utilized, it evoked a visibility in a very dim arena, to make some barely lit opacity recur in a dab of a pale color even as ebony made tired azure go to bed.

I was unaware how a race, colony, pod, or any den of average humanity made homes in aboriginal abodes. If it even elusively were here so removed in a time before now, I had an inability to define, but as I came to notice, Fop Eli was a maven of eras ago. He solely had a nose to dig up aromas of a bit of a civilized abode to nominate some likely native human origin.

In a haze, he deposed in a conovowel usage for us, "Ah. A rib of Adam even Eve never educed. An era cavemen iterated in a few abodes over every rare habitat arose to define man as avatar. A man or a woman, I denote, was an animal of a desire to mate. By nature to have to love, women evaginated an avatar or a god of a human origin. As a holy denizen, an evaginated ape (for a man of a time so far ago was an apelike male) became god in a ceremony made by family dupes. A solo son, as a role, was a super-adored avatar."

Eli here hesitated in a fury to salivate to revise, "But as I divine *here* how it originated, a female holy regularity ruled. A solo female became god of every man, as every woman arose to be her avatar-aside."

"How aged is (or is it a was?) a civilized abode here?" Colonel Ahi solicited.

Eli dug a divot of a mire. He put a bit of it up one nasal orifice.

"Mucus is a delicate natural examiner of age," he let on.

I came to decide he was a fake.

"Mucus or a bogy bug of a bogus onus?" I japed.

Eli made no debate to remedy my defamatory note. He cavitated as a motor in a marina makes a soda-like sud of a dud in a vapory pop of a futility to resonate but operatively make no move.

"His abacus is an elaborate device," Colonel Ahi babysat Eli, but in a tone to deliver a rumor of evocative satire.

Fop Eli resumed an agitated utility. He'd on a dare have had a facile time to come to some fake sum or average nobody'd arise to deny.

"Bak of a tune, nine times eleven, one nine for one's one," he made so finalized a vocality, we were taken in a general avidity to be sated, even ere he came to define no definitive finality.

"Maya numerology? Ha! Bak of a tune, my wet uvula!" Linolena tore. "We're miles afar of any Mexican abode." Her ability to conovocalize came far as it ever on average had. A desire to have more to gag Eli made her elucidate.

So here came her evener Eves.

A mute bit of a manipulated agility let on in a tale no male was aware to decode how every female had a fate to make Fop Eli recapitulate his inane medicine wagon elixir of oratory.

"He's in a fever," Erika put a figurative digit up Eli's anus.

"I'm a cure," Linolena began a line for everybody to resonate to regale some delicate removal of abase laces.

"I'm a cure," rose to some decibel apex as every female rose to ride Fop Eli.

Repetitive, rude, demonic, abusive. to be sure, but everybody was amused, if amok, even Eli.

*

Colonel Ahi had a vital item of a future nature to nominate for everybody to figure: here we were, put in an isolated abode. We defined, as one finality had it, a pat "If" of a set-up, as in, "If I were life's one final man of any virility, do we not (a negative pose made so racily barefaced a bid a mite more polite) have some duty to regenerate future life?"

But in a human abode defined as a colony pod of a fop, a colonel, an amulet acolyte/ marine veteran, aside some women of a homosexy yen, an evocative lure to mate, for any sake, likely was a line no female was one to go for. Overabove, here we were set on a site putatively ruled by an ur epitome. My waves of amulet evocative radar ability were beset in a din of avatar asides.

In a semi-holy visit, an anemonic ukase came to layer a caked edit of animated analysis in a model of a meta-female nag. I was alone beset, as I was of an inability to ban every teletype-likened evocative memo to rile me. Like female relatives in a cabal of ur-originated anima solidarity, my divisive visitor operatives iterated a gamut of adage by mama to wife tales.

"If a baby has a desire to run on a pule jag, I've got a poke to justify misery for a baby."

"Put any cares above base dares."

"If every lad alive met a demise by some dare to hop over a ravine by bike ride, how is it O.K. as a rule?"

"Take however a huge fare ya like, but awarely mop up every bite."

"Defecate not at a locale to dine."

"Do not agitate to wave family linen of a pubic epic."

"Anytime, big ape, give me my wifely fix."

"A fix of a ruby? How abominated a felony was it?"

"I do not of any veracity care. Nude poker is a game

for a Midas of erotic agility. For every body he'd arise to pet is a body to be set as enured as a mineral on ice. Go, have fun."

"One more time late? Fine. Do not imagine my time has any monetary benefit or even a jot of a legitimacy to be honored, as if I were but a robot of a mate, set aside for a duty, solely put on a level as one hired is, if one's a hire for a sum of abuse."

"Hit a gate, mate, do not abide here no more no more no more no more, hit a gate mate, do not abide here no more."

However I made do, my capacity to be given oral-emulated abuse by feminine wiles of avatar aborigines ate my power of ability to refuse.

"Women of ur," I teleposed an ave, "how am I to be fit of use to humanity?"

Babel abated. I but iterated a facile care to be put in a role to do labor.

"Are we to make more humanity? Do we favor a future to live for every woman, every man? Or a future set on a timeline to genocide? Make more women! I have my duty to make more!"

"Be careful, as any bid is a bona fide desire to satisfy," came like some laser in a fired amen of a finale to be resumed.

*

I receded in a dive to some removed arena. By magic, a paranatural agility had eliminated every foregone site to give me some new abode here. Here?

Here was a cave-like foyer in a huge metal edifice. Domicile sides of a mural of an abalone toned opaline patina paneled every façade. To be set amid a mica maze was a ruse to bedevil anybody, but I was elated as one so put upon, as I was evocatively honored as one to be given a role to become. To become how? As a magical aside, my hex abided in a securely tacit operative ruse. To be let in on it at one total episode now evaded any hopes I'd on average have had.

On average, however, I figured an avatar itinerary did evocatively vow an awe to remit any boredom. As a man utility, made to make, did I merit a dukely corona, for I had a fate to save humanity by semen inoculated ekes, one for one by many for any, to donate seminal ovule doses in a pure love for uterine nubile nobility? Nubility! Nubility was a female god of an avatar I came to donate my life for. In a humility to lure favor, I lowered every motive to sate my base desires as I levitated every vagina to populater ace level of a pose to generate some role to be General of a new unit of amino-based acidity.

By waves of evocative power, I made my bid.

A holy ha-ha type tic elucidated a yes, as I decoded it. In a token of a wave to give note, some rare dove made me locate how I'd elude sides of adobe mica murality to deter any move to be made. By alary powered ability, my desire to go made me go for it; one dove did a dip of a hover at an adit, opened in a mute lure. To be yet in a mica-like latitude removed as I was, I saw every here bit as it elaborated a labor arena.

Limited use came to renovate my habitat. A vise based on a lined up axis of an operative facility modulated ecology to befit an economy to manage some deliberate labor of a type for a maker of an ability to do. Motored on a dynamo to facilitate, my line moved one vise to more vises. Every vise had a human anatomy module— not of a vinyl atony but in a natural if anew analogy body to put in a lifelike woman of a robotype man.

A forewoman in a cape to hide her emotive face manipulated a lever as a bow on a lyre for a melody to move vises apace, so some new anatomy laborer alined one more body bit upon in utero, so to vocalize.

"Labor," a female tone came to regulate. My role was a foregone duty: to labor, as a maker of a model of a new age human.

I came to some hereby vise, made my tubed epoxy to put on an anatomical unit. It, an olive/ ruby hematic unit, emulated a core-posited anatomy do-dad, e.g., a liver or a bowel. I was avid in a desire to do my bit, a desire more to not abominate some heretofore done labor of anybody before me.

"Make do, make do, make do, make do."

Like some nubile siren in a rotary baton agility revel or a game pom of a pom agitator of oral avidity, my forewoman iterated inanity, but abuse managed elusively to make me make do, vise to vise to vice to vice.

But as every male to female model of anatomy came by line to my vise, vices of a sexy nature came to me to validate how a bisexed unity came to be fused in every body. My role was one not operatively to make women alone beside men alone but a hema/ demi more like sex Amazon of a dupe lexicon, a ruse to win over a new age humanity by penile/ gynocological unity. Surely, somebody had a gig as a sex examiner, one to rate how every model operated in a capacity to remake humanity?

My amulet acolyte vane to get evocativity was ever a wave-wise radar of ur avatar asides. As I desired a move to be gone, some wise forewoman of ur opened an exit. I had use to do my duty to make more modules of anatomy, but I made more yet if I became go-to man of an elucidator. As I meditated on a nexus, I had an inability to deter an evocative sidebar eke to Fop Eli. My time to be cave maker of operative module humanity had agitated a vibe to retune my sex examiner ad of a vice to lure Fop Eli. So he had a wile to bet.

"As a sir of a vice, my capacity for a mater is a virile cure for any model. I've got a wag of a wager. I can evoke desires in any new age bi-sexy model. If I degenerate to be no fun, I donate my body to however an ur avatar-aside decides a man as I am is of use. To be put in exile, to be set up in a labor? Amen."

A doge made Fop Eli don a toga. For a live sex arena, we had a pit of a river aridity bed amid a bower of ivy covered aromas. Aromas of oregano made me salivate, but any saliva my maw exuded imagined a non-erotic episode. More to relate to toga/ Roman eras, I had a memory to revisit a pit of edacity finality for a fine diner of elite Rome to vomit in, as a natural utile rebuke to forager avarice.

Fop Eli gave his ave for everybody to hale. He gyrated. As a male to be wed is alone before his amore comes at a pace to be delivered as a lure for everybody to covet, Eli capered. Irony led on a line to parody, but Eli faked an unaware disavowal of any capacity to ramify however everybody saw a fop of a male to be. He was in a role to be wed as adored.

A paragon of a model of adulated ability to be mated as a woman or a man of a native verity to mate came to him. A female/male module made by me! So, to win, Eli had a duty to resonate solely not a human anima female/ male but a model of a male/ female figure. Did a bi-sexy robot exude desire, let alone basic ability, to mate? To like love made by some fop? As Eli gyrated a hula to seduce, his operative vagina cum a penis exuded a bemused awe to be so feted. Eli gave her of a him a nip, a pet, a pat, a tip of a lip in a decorum a module likes, if of any desire to be seduced. An evaporative move began in a tone to redo his amore capacity's awe to be done by him.

"Even an anatomical Amazon of ur-avatar ability has an ovulater of a female core to motivate her; likewise, some robot of a he has a core libido makes." Ahi deduced.

As Eli did an amatory homage to love lore no man of average mores abided, every woman—ur-avatar aside, native to woman, or emanated in a vise line, was amused. Eli simulated erogeny to be savored as a joke, not a sexy fix of a mature love but a peg in a hole juvenile rig as Eli made fun of an inability to make his awesome module vagina fit, as it operatively were, her erotica penis. A fit afar, it elucidated a deliberate ban, aware to deny wiles of Onanite fixes, as every bi-sex unity was in a fate to mate side-by-side, face-to-face: not in a parody for a fop.

*

A power of a super ability made me notice how I was in a zone to become degenerated in a rapid atomized exit. In a by-bit, I faded as everybody faded in an image relative to me. Did a body heretofore put on ice have some capacity to go hazy now or one more time? Was I put in a peril as ice cubes are, set in a fire? Nobody came to note how, as Eli bowed, I was erased.

Eliminated in an erasure, my solidity came to refit as a resolute meta-man in a locale removed, a locale like holy paradise, but on a cumulus of an anabatic arena. Here were more vocalized evocative jibes of a holy role, but in a male tone. Were my woman avatar asides amid a male god utility zone? To be removed in a haze was a finality, like demise. Were my feline nine lives up, as in a demise to make me kaput?

If I were done for, I had a so be done set of an avidity to get on it. It, as a paradise/ Hades or any zero time nihility to deny however a man abides . . . I was open.

A vapor ecology divided as a huge divinity rose to become defined as a god, if I were not in a fog. A face saturated an ebony colored image to typify some maw as it evocatively recited an oracular exegesis.

"I by Jupiter am a Jehovah of a Wotan Odin, a Kali Dali Lama Rumi Rama, Rumor of Ali, Monitor of Everyman, Idol of Isis or Osiris as in a divine time to be do-be-do, Demeter in a Hera harem, as a Venus on a Muse jag of a wage to wag; I'm a super ace rarer avis of a Leda womanizer, a Mary Jesus abuser, a dorado deluge for an azure fazed eve, some revery for a reve. We, my divine mates of a holy fate, have rarely noted, in a mere man, a likewise capacity to be divine. But it is a verity, Conovowel Operative, we give ye, based on a life led as a man, a time here, to be tutored as one to behave like we have behaved. As an idol or an avatar aside? Not even. As a god."

I was agog. I had a duty to cede, nod, or aver a desire to be so tutored, or I'd evoke to deny so honored a bid. As a god in a to-be capacity, however, I had a duty to behave now as a divinity behaves.

"I by Jiminy do hereby bow in a yes of a vow as an elite to be so tutored," I delivered a bower of adulative vegetal aromas of a type to betoken a likewise vibe.

My oral ability to cite god-alike legitimacy was a

caricature yet, as I put on a baritone vocality to resonate. Here, however, every cumulus evoked a gym of a locale for any god of a super ability to hone his ace capacity to bedevil. Everybody was in a tutored a là mode mode, to be refit as an up of a to-date model. Every body? No, here were no body-regulated anatomical elites. A many-colored ozone haze defined a super elite denizen. I had, as one to be made by god as a god, a similar atony. My solid anatomy was a goner.

As one to have so lately revisited a yen, I more-to-more desired an erotica fix.

"Ah, it is a desire we god elites abate never," a haze hereby related, in an evoked aside. "To be super is to have forever a desire to solidify bodily, to mate cum every human."

"As a god, one can agilely vary his ability to get it on in any case, no?"

"Some can. I do, but it on average takes a time to peruse how it operates in a move so some divinity becomes aware to do."

"Time we have," some cumulus arose to hover over us.

I had, as anybody'd imagine, many more cares. As a new or a novice god, I more had a care to fit in. As one to have power of an evocative nature, however, I had an inability to hide my cares. Even a minor or average god of any capacity, had a facility to decode my non-isolated uniterated ego motives.

One so minor a care made my divinity mates amused, as I posed a holy note.

"To refer, as one can use, to 'bedevil' as a divine duty makes a paradox of a verity. For an amoral or a moral adage, how are divine fates of awe to be decoded? As evil? As a benefit? Or as a nonalined edit of a savage nature?"

"Yes, a god is as a devil (or a devil, as is). As a devil, a divinity has a duty to bedevil."

"Are we made to define how a god is?" I had an analogy to defer in a memory to, likened in a pat evocativity to games of a divisive nature to vilify some hero, to likewise box or agitate by wily fury for a face-to-face savagery, faked in a role for a moronic ado for amused if abusive rubes in a pit.

As it evoked a by-gone memory, my nexus of images amused every divinity here.

"No. To be god is a fate to be liberated," one had a pity to let on. "It is a fate for a man, of a body limited as a device to be detonated at a time to be done, to cope. For a god, open as a comet of ozone vapor, it is a rule to merely be. For a divinity to be set up or ID'ed as a benefit or evil is a job a busybody has a desire to define."

Many now alit in a line to be named as one god or a set of a divinity. My divine core lore was a joke, set in an unaware daze, so many were new or exotic, even if every divinity here were forever. A wide capacity to fit every civilized arena gave me more god operatives. It emulated a tiny city. Were we to recover a bit of every citizen anybody met in a city?

But a divinity was on a level above mere recon agility level. A god exuded a pure capacity to be polite by rude tenacity. Rudely polite decorum abided in an amity for every denizen. As a "godigy," however (a divinity to be tutored), I was a bit of a celeb or a pet. Every divinity came to me to bid an ave.

Names, I barely noted. Every name but one.

"Satan." A fume levitated in a halo.

*

Were we levitated, on an above level of a refined apex, or abased, in a fire pit of a hole?

"*Divine Comedy*? Ha! *Paradise Gone*? Sure. Level one to nine for a punitive panorama regimen? I dare demur. A holidate parade's a barely more valid analogy to model a divinity zone. We're like huge dilated ozone Bozos elevated up above, roped on utility lines, agilely towed in a row over everybody yet in a set on a lane below. Utility lines of a figurative nature, to simulate human epic analytical acumen."

As a tutor in every divine rite, Satan adored a satirical exegesis. I became his ace pupil.

"One delusive coda by human opined analysis is a desire to define by sex, e.g., am I male?" he regaled. "In a type, yes; in a type, no. Bi-sex or as a more likely poly-sex or even as a no-sex icon, I have to be. To facilitate human analysis, I go by male nominatives. It is a lazy but a facile mule to ride. However, I have capability to be female, male, however I come to be."

He had a likewise facility to ride to define divine validity: by negatives. I noted awarely how every verity he gave was in a negative definitive tone. He'd elucidate how it is agilely not as a fate come to be but as a fate likely never in an age to be. Holidate parade *Divine Comedy* rebukes? I was abused as an amuser of a divine devil. A hazed amity made me game for it. As I was in on it, a levity developed.

I made him arise to refute more takes on a negative paradise basis.

"In a recital of a tale, my memory poses a hetero/ homo male/ female/ female caricature mix-up, as everybody did adore somebody not of any desire to love her or him. A hetero male loved a homo female, homo female loved a hetero female, hetero female loved a hetero male fixed on a homo female: *Not an Exit*."

"As any divinity'd aver, it is a deluded exegesis of a non-exit. As a divinity, ya have divine rites of amore. Women or any men are fare game. We love humanity forever as a god, in an erotica zone."

"Time was, a fabulosity had a Satan or a devil in an aside put a bid on a body to give his emotive holy core to Satan, in a sale to take finality. So, to some medicine man, in one case, many pages opined in awe how one can evocatively waver in a hate to decide how a future to get every luxury now is a totality to remit as a forever of utility for a devil."

"One more morality tale. How is it a raw utility for a man of a fate to have had any luxury to be forever in a divine capacity to bedevil? As anybody can avow, it is a job a fine many rise to homicide for."

"In an era far ago removed, I perused a novel of a name like *Family Karamazov*. In it, an episode had a devil or even a namesake Satan of a bedeviler, a figure to justify war, agony, misery, rot, et. al., as a fate made by some divine logic. I have but a hazy memory to revisit it. It elucidated evil as a fate we have to have, to live humanely. Was it a fake memory? Did it arise to define fate, evil, as a divinity defines it?"

"I liked it. As a made-by-man exegesis, it alined in a rage to befit one likely telegony to sire some son of a moronic if imaginative logic. Even if any memory here to revisit it is a ruse to defy validity, he had a nice go to get it in a lively debate."

"Many televised episodes of average life came to run amok in a nuke war. A solitary loser of an everyman abided in a locale wiped of any humanity by an atomic eraser. At one take, he has a fine time. Here's a bonus of every delicacy we're likely to desire: wine, tuna, game hen, avocado pate, rosemary sage tapenade for edacity; jade, ruby, dorado carated ice for economy; no fate to remit or elegy to serenade for a bygone race. He's an eremite for a finite forever on a site for avarice's average vices. As it ages, anybody becomes isolated in a desire to do some job, any job, of a generative nature. So his one-time paradise becomes a negative zone, a pit of a holy hole."

"Negative paradises are typical as anyone tires of a locale, regularity, rut, or even an Eden. I'm aware how it arises in a lore to legitimize morality, to make men abide by rules of a regime made for abusive papal elites. A fabulized epic of avarice gone bad is an adage for a wide many native zones. I do not in any case deny how anybody can operate so deluded as a rube to be duped. A divinity has a duty to dupe. Negative paradises are fit as any con is a fine game to sate some yen of a rube for a moral of a punitive morality set-up."

"Are we," my divine solidarity gaped open a civility gap, if any god arose to defy me, "made to bedevil as a duty? Can a divinity refuse to do duty?"

"We can abide however a desire makes us abide, but I'd operate to do some bit of a divine gig, if I were new or on an acolyte level."

I bowed in an agility to befog any cumulus irony. To beg as an acolyte divinity for any more Satanic asides abused a rite, my ruminative nature made me figure. Hazed as a new abuser, I had a duty to devise my very sole role to make men examine life's elusive magic.

*

As a devil-educated acolyte god, I made do to bedevil any men I'd abuse, but I had a mobility fix. I was a novice, as afar as agility was useful. As a fog or an anabatic odor of a vapor, I moved as an ameba, by fake pod overage to go here to yon as if in a desire to be deliberate, wise, careful, or in a merely wavered atony to be hazy. To visit any nominated everyman, I had a line to take. So, to dare my new amebic agility to move how I desired it agilely to move, my focus alit on one zone.

But, up in an ozone layer, I rode far above my resided abodes. As a nod of a care to my bygone times, I figured Ahi was a mate made to be bedeviled, or even Eli. To locate my late sited abode was a basic exam I had a desire to get over.

As I gazed on every locale below, I saw a few alone, some family-like bases, a city, more desolate zones of a nature foreboded as it ever exuded a cumulative degeneracy. To gaze below, I saw I had an ability to go, to be put in an exuded edited exit as I delivered a wad or elixir of a divine haze to be taken on a line to a sited amen.

A solitary man, an Arab or a Semite caveman of a man in Oman or a like-sited arena, noted a holy visit of a divinity was up as I was exuded in. As an everyman in a loco daze, he was a fine figure to begin a new avidity/ religulosity for everybody to bow in awe to. He wore robes of a nude mole hide. He bared an agony by soles of ebony pedicured in a pit of a tar ecology. Razored as a military tabula rasa, his age-savaged onyx adobe nut of a pate had a patina for a mite colony to sabotage.

But I had, as in a time before, to defer awarely to how I was on a pace to relate my holy parole so he'd evocatively get it. Aha, some divine tip arose to let on: a divinity had an ability to relate to men of a misery to hope for a divine yo! However I made my desires evoked, anybody so put upon as a lone denizen in a zone for a bare luxury was open as a dupe for any notes a holy moly divinity delivered, in any Babel.

I vocalized in, as a devoted editor adores evoke, "holy parole palates" of a nature conovowel is agile to simulate. Palaver exuded as an elixir of an oracular ado to make my rube venerate me. He bowed, ululated in awe to bow one more time.

Not a bad alakazama to deliver, if I do rate my capacity to be divine, for a novice god.

Ilalila was a name to go by. My man, at any rate, raved a moniker as Ilalila. My name was One to Be Holy, so to put it. Or, if it arose to be, we were set in unanimity to have same names, I was Ilalila to him.

One memory by my bygone time revisited an American awe, some religulosity named as a Momon or a Moron? A con of a renegade put a Jesus era revery to base his iconic aleluja jujus of a holy sanitized elegy date later. It on average came to him or any male to be fit in a web of a wed erogeny to have many wives.

As a god, I figured a sugary rebate made religulosity more fun. I herefore let Ilalila have my holy votive liberality to do however a male desires, if a male made some bow in awe to do my divine rites. I made my regime negatively model a regular usage many jujus in a veto mode did. I figuratively gave him a tabula for a tome to tote to relate my rules of every vital itinerary:

No sodomy but in a human anus, as an animal is a mate for an animal ewe love.

No beverage but ale.

No war of any type, but a game can arise to wage some war of amity.

No fare but a delicacy ruminated in a refinery by cud of a bovine.

No tolerated avidity for any yuletide homily.

No tame pet of average ferocity.

No pipe, cigar, or a toke by vegetative bane but as a sedative to make revery.

My No's enumerated at a holy seven, I retired. Awed, Ilalila bowed. I had a care to note how an eremite here was a veteran of a capacity to pare many a divine delivery. He'd abide by some holy law or ukase, to take deliberate time to go for a divinity bid of a base likely to lure popularity. No lame novice god acolyte had a hope to motivate some fanatic operative to begin a denominated evocativity to regulate lives.

Or, I had a dare to veto, more likely some rube here was a tipover of a dupe for any divinity to manipulate.

But, in a move to move him, I had one more bit of a holy note to deliver, as I made vocal avocatory havoc in a serene fury.

"Beware. Ye have to do some job no Job ever in agony had a care to do: to facilitate delivery for a woman of a love for a divinity like me. To locate her, arise to go to some colony zoned in awe for an Amazon amity. Here, ye have to be met as one to be fit as a fuse for a Japanese colonel, Ahi by name. So Colonel Ahi can arise to have ye lit in a fire for one Fop Eli to detonate to liberate my love."

Sure to run up a totality, he duly began a pile to venerate me, by lapidary masonic ability to set up an idol. I was one made god.

*

One facet of ecology here, by divine rule, was a new (as I saw it) ability time had as episodes eked an era. Time here delivered episodes at a same time, forever, as every bit of a tale come to be/ came to be had at one time come to some visitor or at one more time to somebody removed in a remote zone. Had I lived on as a man, I'd, on average, have had an inability to visit an episode, however, at any solitary time. But as a god, I visited any times I desired, amid a given episode.

So, my seminal evocative yo to my human idolizer Ilalila had operatively developed a rage my holy rule had unawarely fixed. Ilalila now (if any "now" is a validity) had arisen in a role to become some Peruser of a Divine Nature. Modeled as an avatar, Ilalila had a power of a demagogic abuser. I was, as irony made me, his ability maker. I made him a juju mojo domo by my divine nexus.

I was a bit agitated. Images of a holy role gone bad inanely made my divine debut a joke. Satan, as every divinity, had a levity fit.

"Every fate's a dice game," he deputized any bet as a move for a game life made.

Some Taliban or a similar avidity revoked every civility to run amok as an epidemic. Everybody was agog in a race to be punitive to sub-elites. A sub-elite was anybody to hesitate to venerate me (god as I was in an idol analogy).

Were Fop Eli, Colonel Ahi, my women of Amazon in a zone hereby? More men of a raved esoterica were rife, some women abided in a basic abase role level, as more men of an elite level abused any denizen of a lower emotive role. Riled emotively by vocal ability, some rose to be top as a dog is a top in a bow of a wow.

One more capacity my divine nature gave me was an ability to forage by visibility to notice somebody put in a pen of a den of a penal arena. No site rose to hide some man in a covered-up abode so no divinity saw.

A forage visibility, like divine mobility, was a labor I labored at in a dire desire to do before capacity to be facile came to me, but I did.

A side bonus of a simul-every-zone visibility set in, as a lot of images at one time came to me, to layer upon images of any item I saw or imagined. In a move to mime how I came to note time, my race to visit in a visibility forage mixed every bit I saw. I was one deliberate to take more time to decode how an image fit a fare before. To be dutiful, I'd emulate my god operatives in any divine forage to focus on one desired unit or unity.

By to by, herefore, lasered images, imagined or as is, elucidated awarely to be focal, as if a mere hope had a power evocatively to make valid any desire. Colonel Ahi sat on a cot in a meditative pose. Fop Eli wove to hop in a regimen of acatatonic exile to be fit as a man is abusively made to be, put in a can of a pen. Isolated as an edited unit, Ahi cum Eli were, per one take, honored as itemized in a set a god exiled aside. My man Ilalila had operatively managed a site to fit in. As a holy role mole, he'd abide by my law.

As awe came to him, any hereticality was evocatively valid, if it arose to him as it (or, as if it) operatively were. He decided, as a nexus on a divine/ human axis, every databyte to mitigate how a city model operated. A huge modicum of edacity gave him a capacity to revise definitive holy rule so he'd alone be fed a rare cut, above culinary fares of average men. As ace Peruser of a Divine Nature, he had a final edit on any holy law I'd, as a divinity, have given, in any vocal asides I'd evoked.

Ahi cum Eli were, herefore, put on ice for a bit as Ilalila figured a role for anybody so nominated in a divinity's amen. I, however, saw one menace hover as a move to be made: to give live votive human anatomy to me, for every future surety.

"Ho-ho!" Satan, amid a divine din, elucidated a fate my panic icily foreboded: any mused aside by me was evocatively given as a divine duty to be done by him, Ilalila. Before, so to pose, he was unaware; now, as it ever is, Ilalila had a duty: to give me my men, as oxen or ewes are given, in a votive cut.

Agog, I was as of a time yet, a god, or at any rate, some godigy. My power of a divine type had a bit of a bite, no?

"Do not agonize. Time for a divine pop-in," I gaveled as a magus.

"A divine pop in?"

"A divinity motor, as in a comedy. Some diviny'd arise to pop in a comedy to save somebody so he'd arise to get over a malady."

"Comedy's an analogy. Here we defy life."
"Defile?"

*

Define divine defy defile: however it abusively resonated, I had a duty to deny fates I had evoked in a fever of awe my panic elevated as I telexed a lazy notice to my notary cop Ilalila. But, as I was educated, a divinity had a limited ability to vary how a man awoke to god-evoked avocatory waves. Any comedy decided in a finale by some tidy, pat amen is, as any divinity related, a made-by-man opus.

A divinity did awarely have, however, an awe to leverage how a man operated. Agog, Ilalila was in a tone to be tuned in an avidity by me. But, I wavered in a dare to care, were my fated asides, every final one, done? Some positive line to go fore to likely futures? A negative line to some done to-do rose to make me verify how every finale came to be. Yet on average no finale was a final, as a wide delivery menu more widened.

"Every pare has a bi-l of an el of a level aware to bare," Satan arose to relate, by conovowel usage, how elusive side-by-side lines of a locomotive line never are to be met, in an image to validate how a likely fate becomes an "if" of one beside more likely fates, at a same time. By mitosis, a divide makes a side-by-side body.

So, my sole hope was a care to secure some fate to give my mates a solace, to secure some repose. Here, more super-adiposed images ate to become fat in a lipidity to saturate visibility mirages. Every fate hid in a fused edacity to lap over imagined images of any more to be done. My god ability had a care to limit any vile fates. As I made my desire resolute to ban agony, however, a panorama came to me. To wit, I saw a man over a fire on a pike, some hose water up a nose, more rot of a gut abuse by tiny cut isolated in a saline kin on a nap of a nip or a savagely lacerated itinerary to tap every bit of anatomy sap, an acidy mace to bone to saponify human anatomy bit of a by-bit at a time. More fates of agony came to me. Fates I'd ere never imagine were to bedevil everybody. Human anatomy votives of agony paled, as if in a game, beside so many more vile finales.

Ilalila was ever awed in a more fused of a con agitative nature. My misery catalog overage gave him, a mere man, a fare to gag on. Every likely demise his enemy had a fate to face was abuse he liked, in one role, to validate. Yet, it arose to him, as I gave him a nip, as a holy nexus of a juju mojo domo, *he* had a duty to validate by *his* owed agony. To be decapitated as a man is a power a solo holy role model alone can awarely generate. *He* was one to be set in a focus of agony.

"To become verily holy, man is examined in agony to be Son of a God," I repetitively derived a religulosity model everybody was in on.

Agog in awe, however, Ilalila saw it as a new arisen isodynamic icon of a votive to redo how a man alit upon an epitome.

Satan, et. al., agitated a bit. If I were to give my man a token of a divine nature to be let in, upon a holy role to be forever elevated as a god acolyte, he'd abide here. Nobody here liked Ilalila. He was a fanatic, a man-o-war, a piker of a pirate god; a fake, sure, but a fake to con a rare few. As a divine ravenosity came to caw at any move to let Ilalila become holy, some did elucidate how I solely had a duty to *give* hope. To *deliver* on any hope was a fate no divinity like me had a duty to do.

"Give more, yet in an amity to be given as a wafer. I give ye me by wafer as a token of a holy take. Take my wafer as an analogy to be me, yes as I give to ye my wine to be me by token as an ave to some kin of a den. I come, cum unity, Mary me, my winery to be."

"Holy Jesus on a pole!" gave him a name.

Satan arose to relate how a Son of a God of a divinity had a 'tude we cynical or un-united in any hope for average humanity divine types eluded. A Jesus operated on an Ave Mary level as one yet in a haze to rule by some fine role, but it as a rarity made him emulate somebody typical as an ire-dire-fire god.

"I like him O.K. On average, he's a nice divinity, but up on a cumulative level, a rife many come to rile. We tolerate him. A few are finer as a very rare minority. To let in one more son of a god is a move more popular as a gale to raze solid edifices of an amity we like to have. We are forever, are we not? In a forever arena, we have to be careful of any new or any radical agitative figures."

One Jesus or one son of any god is a limit, every divinity decided.

"I got it," I bowed. As I had a negative homage to

honor Ilalila—besides, a more vital emotive desire to save Colonel Ahi, Fop Eli—some fake bid of a divine role for Ilalila was a resolute fate. "But," I had a care to rale, "do we have to monitor Ilalila's agony?"

"Ha! Let 'im agonize to rot alone."

*

For a panorama, Satan enumerated a set of imaginary futures Ilalila had: as a holy fake, rex of every vex, avatar, acolyte to some vile vicar, or a pope named Amos Uno. Colonel Ahi, Fop Eli, besides any renegade women of Amazon avidity, were liberated, as an agape lot of Ilalila's operatives, in agony, bore how Ilalila became some derivative Jesus of a holy sore lode fanatic.

I came to refute my move to bedevil any man. Ilalila, before my divine poke, was a nobody for anybody, but as I gave him a role to cop as a nexus of a divinity, he did an Icarus, arose to be set afire, lit in a fury by sun of a god as if in a fury by god of a son. Even as an acolyte god, I was one tired abuser.

"Are we god acolytes of any divinity not in a site to vacate duty, to relax as a man on a side to take some time to get over every labor?"

"A made god is a god of a non-average yet a non-elite genesis. A native god is an average yet an elite case, to have lived, as it operatively were, forever. As a god of a tale related in an awe to give some human or animal a divine finery, ye have more to do. We natural elites in a holy role have fewer axes of a figurative divine nature to hone to raze some lot of a human ecology," some huge cumulus of anabatic agility posed a tenet I was aware to take for a rule. Made god or "average" native god, I was one divine figure, no?

My wary negativity came to my nemesis in an evocative jab. I had a natural ability to rile demagogic agas, I did aver, in a mute but eked emetic of an ire to gag a god.

"I give how an acolyte takes. If I desire to revoke how any mere man is one so given in a holy sinecure to sin as a god, I have power of a divinity to sever every divine line to him."

As a mere man, I had a humility to be politic if a god arose to rebuke me, but here, remade to be set up as a holy figurine to mimic a god, I was in an awesome fury to become somebody to refuse rebukes any divinity had a care to make.

Besides, I had an eligibility to cite how I came to be put in a divinity set-up. In a tidy many holy zones, a tiny demerit or a puny gap of ability did edit a man on a divine visit. Even a bona fide holy divinity had a care to be careful, as a wily many got ejaculated in a hobo's exit if a more major elite divinity had a desire to ban any figure figured as a bane. To come to go, to be mobile, was a definitive divine fate for a holy level.

If I were bad as a god, I'd agitate some suped up epitome god. An exile to some lower arena was a likely future to finalize my holy role. To rile divine civility, herefore, became my hope to get a life.

Life? How ever in any case did I desire to revisit a time my life had abided in, or even a time heretofore not abided in a life yet of any set use to me? Were men of anatomy given a divine refuge typical in a desire to be delivered as any god-educated avatar acolytes on a revisited utility to be wise? To live lives over, one more time, wised up in a holily tutored amity was a sinecure to rival a divine gig. As a man aware to be wise to how a life/ demise/ holy con operated, I'd elusively have some pat amity core to put every malady misery memory to bed. Elated as an alated ibis of a holy deliverer, I'd abide to be some pure paragon of ominosity to forebode how a life can arise to honor every divine ga-ga ca-ca.

To be some roper, a sales operative for an in of a side game was in one role, were my life to be remade human. As a human of a divine savory fare surety to be hip, I'd emulate a mad eremite. To be taken as a nut of an Ilalila was a cover any divinity type to come to redo his alive life time had a fate to face. To be so typed, I'd arise to cover any cabala-like code lore my god elites in a cumulative hegemony had a desire to hide.

"No," Satan emanated in a gas.

"Are no divine codes or any holy lore to be hid in a haze so men are set in an unaware capacity to figure how it is?"

"I care not. Abovemore, divinity cares are not of

a nature men are let in on. Even an acolyte like ye, given a visa here, can agilely have no capacity to focus or ability to verify how, or if, a divinity cogitates or operates. I can aver, as a totality, we have no solicitudes, as afar as any man imagines. On a same topic, every care ye have, comes evocatively to me. So bored, I've many times abided in a levity to tolerate how any come to desire some limit as an avatar or acolyte god. It is a regularity to have men inanely figure ruses of a type to con a god."

Apologize to Satan? As I cogitated it, it amused every divinity here. Likewise, my desire to go met a positive divine vote yes, if any vote were to be taken.

I had a care to meditate how I'd emanate to revisit a life time. To be remade by divine rite to model a duke? Some popular amatory reveler? A famed operator in arena games? A wise curator of enological elixir? A political usury leverager of a ruler everybody loved? An ace race wagerer? A comedy banana to top any cinema-based id of a base hilarity?

Somehow, an itemized edit of a fine many human ados opened, in a panorama to give fame to my life.

"Typical," a divine vocality barely hid a satiric amen. "Every man arises as a famed ace to revisit as a hero. Lives are like reves, in a delusive finery to give men a nice time."

*

Time was, a nice time was a nice time. Time came to me repetitively layered, as one more memory reset as an afore-fate literary device to deliver anybody to some time to sit on a meter, at a site to be taken as a vital arena for a future to nominate for a notability. No memory had I to cite how a device to time-deliver anybody here to yon ever alit any man in a locale to have no vital ado to relate how an era had arisen as an era to note. To wit, if a time-delivered everyman alit on a time set in a war arena, he came to be set amid a havoc of a fury he'd ere perused of in a tome—not at a site removed afar. Every time so noted in a novel iterated a time to be noted.

In a redux of a life, however, a time delivery device had on average no role to put a man in a war or any famed era. Herefore, to be reset in a life gave me hope to be put in a time my heretofore life had abided in. A nice time.

Yet, I had abided in a few arenas of agony, times I'd as ever as any time have some desire to now elude. Did I have power, as a meta-man of an acolyte divinity, to be put in any definite locale? To focus on a definite locale was one power I had, I hoped. It emulated a lasered amen I'd used as a god acolyte to make my lunatic Ilalila behave. But, as it evocatively came before to waver, I'd imagine my site to vary now.

An analogy to recur iterated a focus I'd evasively set up: a casino came to regulate how everybody got a time to be put in any site. Likely zones of a desired abode came to go, to vary by sites of abodes I hated as I recovered abodes I'd abovemore foreboded in an omen of a revery to be reposited in any locale below.

A desire to be likewise liberated, in an ability to mobilize my life site to site, per any moves I'd arise to make, came to me. To be put in one zone forever? I never imagined it. If I were to be made to live, my fate had a future fatality to take me. So any forever, as in even a fine fate to be put in a paradise, became not as abovemore desired as a demise type finality.

To be given ability to be how I desired in a life to be was, I decided, a hope—not a verity. Some god, even an acolyte divinity, had a vote/ veto power over a fate to be given. Alive, my divine power or ability was inutile. But, I'd as of a yet of a future, have wise power. As one to have wise power, of an ability to be wise to holy codes, I'd arise to be sedated in a lazy pax axis of amity.

"He deliberates as if a fate were not one decided ago."

"He was a dud in a divine run. Acolytes, even evocative-powered ones, are typical aloha cases. As in a rapidity to be gone."

"Forever is a time he has a gap of any to no time to figure."

"Like so many men."

"Even as an acolyte to be divine, he never awarely got it."

"If it were a facile gig, anybody'd arise to become holy."

"We have some fun of a future nature he can arise to like."

"Defer any related aha!"

"Sure, but as an evoker of emanated ado, he can ape to beware. Now even, every bit I relate can emanate to him."

"It is of use to nobody to be tuned in, even evocatively, to divinely deliberated ominosity. We can emanate however elaborately we desire to give some bit of every refined aware note, but a totality yet is a definitively bare face a divine code hides: e.g., as I now orate, he's avid in a desire to be tutored as one to be delivered on an exuded aloha to life. Many paces are to be taken in a move to make him alive. So many, he can evocatively never arise to get every bit. I'd aver, if I relate more, he can on average solely come to be more fused in a con of a fuse to be lit."

I got it. As I was in on a heretofore posited exit of one to more delivery fates, I did elucidate some tenet, in a move to define life. Life's animated in a panorama. Humanity's a life model of a relatively minor arena.

More rumored evocativity came to haze me, but I cohered an itemized elegy to my divinity "life" to make time go by. To be sure, few asides of a holy life were times I pined in a desire to relive. To have no body, to move by gas exuded amebic agility, to make some fanatic eremite begin a holy lore con of a religulosity, to decide fate, to have Satan or any likewise divine raja for a mate, to be given any woman or everyman as a cup or a cake were but a many bites I had an edacity for as I rose to forego so set a fare bonus.

As an adage put it, everybody has a desire to go to paradise; nobody desires a demise.

So, however I'd ride to my fate, my desire was a done sale.

*

Before my delivery came to revisit as a man alive to my body, my time, my zones of a solidity figure to be figured, I had one more divine ceremony to revel in, an homage to honor a role taken in acute fame by Jesus, one did aver in an aside to me: to revisit a final aloha he had in an episode to dine before he got abusively riveted, up on an ex of a bar, as ace hole Roman ediles emulated a lice colony to savage him in an agony vise for a vile humility he bore for a holy job. Imagined as a mural as operatively done by some rare colorizer, it evoked a popular arena set up. As a gala, so set a get-up amused everybody here.

Roles of analogy were given. One was a Judas. One became Peter. As one to be delivered, I had a duty to be Jesus. In amity, we humored oratory Jesus: as a role, he had a duty to recite his orated aloha, to set up every ceremony gag. Even if it elucidated every line he had ever exuded as a divinity here, we were saturated as any rube dupes in a love to be saved in every role to ham it up.

On one vital item of a ceremony to dine was a duty we made to fake bites of a fare. No fare was in any zone here. No pig or abalone, no bananas or any taco, tamales, or olives. I salivated, ate by bites of ozone for an epicure finery. Some rake made me lave his evocatively bare soles as in inane levity he faked a sip of a wine.

My Judas operative came to give me his aloha lip amen amenity, to digitize my role to be later a human ewe for a votive demise. How ironic, I meditated as one to begin a redone life, but it emulated, in one tale, how a man (one Jesus) arose to be divine. To get a life by demise had a time-honored agility.

"Now, I cite for one to be me," Jesus arose to give my lines in an evocative poke, so my vocality redid it.

"Amen, every man of a me-my-mo-mum, I hereby decimate, ye have to be mine to go net every man as everyman, as every woman or even as an animal in open ozone saline water. As I depose, ye get a net, operate to become some humanity heron, a rarer avis of a watery zone to take man as a Dover of a sole dove to dive to be boned. As I have boned a Mary, men, I've zoned a many zany denizen."

I was agog as one to relate how I gave vocality to Jesus in a role to be some holy dupe. Yet it amused every god, even awesome Jesus, as I gave my Babel. It evocatively came to me how, as one to come to life by caravan of a demise wagon, I'd emulate some holy mule, some he-haw editor of every saw a holy zoner evoked. I had a rap of amity to ratify.

"Take some raw animal of a pit. It is of a desire not of edacity nor of avarice to be fed or operatively to be fed as a fine fare, to bare be cute, cut a baby to Solomon as I vacate verily, let every baby come to me, for any to not ever in an age have sin is a rote to hone for it is a Leviticus of avidity how I let a haricot of a harelet of a hare lot on a fur of awe to honor or avow as a purity to do how I vow in a body to be, to take my body for an ovine ba, ba, ba."

"Ba, ba, ba," began a general asinine tune, to regale Yale men in a sugary sap of a coda some cinema had exuded.

As every divinity waged a baritone-toned open ozone volume war on any musical ability, fidelity, notes, or agility, my meditative banality let in a desire for a religulosity no Jesus idolizer or even a Jew of a more secular edited avidity had ever abided in. I desired a side regime to facilitate my revisited exit as I remade my life: some Zen or a hen of a hin of a do, some poly divinity set-up or an Ali basic ado, teneted on a Koran or a Kore. Were my roles even in a fix as everybody's inanely to be fixed in awe to some divinity? To be human is operatively to meditate. To meditate makes one to be set up aware, to figure how a human operates as a man is one given in a role to live by some holy rule.

Some game divided ecology types as a vegetative,

mineral, or animal as one posed a poser of a taxonomy refinery for a decoder awarely to define. To begin, one to decode was given a type. To wit, "animal."

Or, one to pose began, "I've cogitated up an item."

"Is it animal, or of a nature more vegetal or of a mineral," a rote ceremony covered an open if one-sided usage for a decoder.

If a type were "mineral," every bit of ecology to be defined as a non-animal or a-vegetal item arose to be named, if one were to decode some poser a poser arose to pose. Many ruses of a binary nature were likely to be put in: e.g. a vegetative savage, like some Venus agape to bite lice was a popular one.

To bide time for a bit as one made to be Jesus in a mural opus, I revisited inane games I'd one time had a desire to do. We were, god or acolyte, game-gone, set on a ride to have some fun.

In one relaxed amuser, I hid. As a rule, we hid one by one, for one somebody to recover. In a game named as I Hide, my role was a more basic one. To be hid in a vale, pit, or any locale for a time many minutes above more made my date. Covered in a hole by some refuse, my locale made me safe. Safety was a care for any kid. I'd imagine my hole gave me forever a time to be put in a vagina. To be sure, my before-pube life gave me no vagina hopes as a per of a se, but I later imagined it as a vagina revisit of a hope to be put in a pit, as I had unawarely hid. At a time heretofore, my sole solo care was a care to be fit in a hole to befit a fit-in ability, to be agile, to have fun as I saw it eliminated a tidy many cares.

Anyhow, I came to, to recover a role here to be put in an opus of a divine game. Jesus alit upon a remark over a wave to deliver a saw I saw as a homily to live by, but I had imagined a banality, to note how every divinity gave nod.

I waved, every divinity waved. As a goner, I came to be delivered.

I now am of a care to relate how a body becomes
a new anatomy model.
   Ovid

As I raged in a fit of agitative reves, I woke to become set in a carapaced anatomy, to be some huge bug. At any rate, I was of a size to hover over a tiny bug. I posited an ovipositor of a capacity to deposit ovi for a colony.

Here we were many, but I was, as I saw, a lone female/ male rex of a colonizer in a body to rule my bug agora. Here? Here was a zone below a canopy below a layered edit of a vegetative viridity. How it, as an ecology, fit in a more major arena was a poser. Any size to size meter of analogical ability was inoperative here. We were colonized as an isolated unit, in a new abode for one set up as I was, in a carapace body.

None came to rile me. My mates elusively gave me more fare to be mine. My fare was a sup of a tiny pedicule, some delicacy for every bug of avidity to dine for. I was evasive but ate, to be decorus as a jejune bug of a colony ruler. It, as a fare, had an edibility to savor, I came to note. Before, refined as a man of an epicure, my palate was one to gag over a sup of a pedicule; now, as a bug, I revised any culinary desires I had ever exuberated in.

Alive to be lively, my carapace waved in a move to regale my new amigos or agile bug operatives. I, however, abided alone, beset in a mum arena, put amid a lot of agitative mite mutes of a capacity to labor as I deposited ovi. We were fit in a hived unit, in a move to make do, but I made no more cajolery to relate to my mates. Even evocativity met a jam of a pure pale sonic erasure.

Taxonomy became vital, as I had a care to define my new etymology. How in a colony here were we bug operatives of usage to be defined? Odonata? Nematode? Were we cicadas, or I.D.ed as a lepidop or a dip, a hymenop or a homop or a hemip, an isop or a mecop or a zorap of a tera coda, to legitimize however a conovowel usage put it? As a tera, tera, tera . . .

Taken as a tip atop, "tera" began a parole to become "teratology," id. es., an academy logy to cover any demonic animal anatomy model. I was, I came to let on, one demon of an atypical emotive/ cogitative/ body sum.

As a tegula for a rugose coxa lobe came to be sutures at a jugal apex, an apodeme domen of a poly-faceted ab use foregut over an agamic or a heterogamic imago's ovipositor amid a bipedate coxa leg atop a fine femur agility to set at a basal apical if in an anal uropod analogy coda. Capitate file nodes on a pilose carina to ride my carapace came like some colon of a do-do to-do to defecate gas of a fecal ejaculatory nature so my ligulate gena to gula to lora by tylus-agape buca generated a docile, wan amity. Humeral acerose setate to setulose hamuli paraded laminated, in a mesad or a mesal on a meson (as a mesamere) homodynamic agility to simulate some tegula jugum of a lobelike lateral élan. As if in a nod of a metazonite coda for a polypede, my coda had a nasutus aloha to taper in a bow. An elite pupa parasite type rode my pedicel, as a pelagic arena remora had utility to benefit a mako. By some retina-likened aparatus of agility, my pedicel arose to take subocular arenas in. As a subimago has a watery debut of an exit, I had a taxis of a desire to become teneral as one to have some new elite body type. But I was, as a totality (not in a hoped avidity to be final) a bug.

*

I did as a bug alone pine for a mate—not a mate for a body to manipulate but one for a mere bit of amity gab. As a heretofore human, I likely was one put in a role to rule here. Were more heretofore human exiles in any likewise roles, amid enemy hives? If, as a hive, we were to become huge, were we fated as a colony to defy some rival? As a ruler, I'd operate to be top enemy gun; or, as a ruler, I saw I'd a duty to hide to be posited in a safe haven, as every bug I deposited ovi for evoked a desire to save me. To cede, my capacity to repel any bug enemy was at a puny level, as I was a novice to manipulate my new anatomy.

But, if in a to-do, we were to come to defy some bug enemy colony, my likely sole time to be met as a human exile by some likewise human exile came to hover. I hoped in a fit of inanity, to relate to him as one ruler of an exile to some likewise human exile: we had a fate to divide, to savor, even.

As one huge bug amid a mum unit, I was alone to figure how every regimen operated. In any case, no god or edit of a holy memo came to give some tip of a regime federated amen I, as a bug aga ruler of an ovipositor on exude duty, had operatively to do, make, set, or, evocatively, make do. Herefore, my duty was a liberated one. No rule ruled any duty for a bug elite to do. My law as a rule was a law of a remote zone, some bad arena for a feral abuse to forage savagely.

So life here was on a monotone note. We recuperated in use to generate more bug ovi by my baby maker ovipositor as I was operatively fed. In one memory so far afar, I relived an aha to define how a man is of a basic avidity to do some types of a generative labor. An abase Hades (as a holy haven is in a likewise fix) is an arena no labor is in a fate to be done. But if I were to be here, set up as a bug in a forever utility to deposit ovi, how are (were, was, is) any regimes of abode, life, labor, et. al., any viler, in analogy, to relate to some bedeviled abider in a hole like Hades? Any forever, if on average bad or unimaginatively fine, was a fate for a loser, I had iterated. As one to have desired a lifetime for a generative labor, I was in a hog abode to live huge my reve.

Were my mere desires, every final one here, to be validated? I solely had a care to hope. So far, one lifetime led a fate to some future life. Future by some gig I'd imagine to become mine to have!

Sure to now, a hubub of a fury got every colony denizen up in a pose for a war. A sonic alarum of a tone made by femoral agitated agility had a vim of ominosity for animosity. No later in any time to mobilize, we were set upon in a to-do, to simulate how I'd imagined an enemy colony to beset us.

As ovipositor elite rex, I was amid a refuge, piled up in or on a tower of a reticulate calyx. I had a general ocularity to take how every saber ace rode to pare rival abuse. My bug operative base was avid as a rabid abusive canine barony to repel enemy venom. As it opened, a van of a wave came to forebode more dehumanized animosity to come. Mites as a picador unit operated on a punitive—not a matador/ executive—level of ability. Many were facilely wiped aside by my bug acid exuder aces, as a toxicity vapor executed a curare fury to defy mere mites.

Over every row, I gazed evocatively to make nexus as a human exile to my rival in a likewise human exile. He'd, I did opine, have his evocative radar up, in a desire to be met as one more human in a carapace cage. We'd, as elites in a wise docility, moderate to fix a pax upon any pox of a war. As a new unit of a bifid or operatively bilateral agility, we'd avow a royal amity to power as a bug axis. As an axis, a bifid unit of even average fury had a leg up on any canopy rival. Anon I saw a future for us of abovemore power, as every colony we met adulated us . . . or, as an enemy, became fixed in a fate for a gory demise.

By some by, my wiry wave got an emanated aloha. Humanity was apace here! Visibility was at a low ability for an anatomy so set up as I had operatively to have, but I made do to define my rival of a ruler, in a like-modeled anatomy. Huge like me, he waved a leg or a pod in ironic amity. We were yet a separated unit amid a bug animosity war. Irony did unite ruler elites as everyman-aborigine types agitated abase for us.

"Ave, my pal of a ruler of enemy colony," lasered in a wave to my rival aga, "My Agamem of a non enemy man exiled in a bug anatomy by some savage god or an average dog in a fate to be boned alone."

"Man alive by body bug, I 'sume, fate's a bone for a *woman* alike to pine for," I definitively got in an evocative wave. So xenomodeled it arose to me to have some woman in a rival enemy pose, let alone some conovowel-evoker of one, my lasery waves emulated an adulative vibe like love. Loves at one lasered ave wave were rare. Yet even abovemore rare were loves in a bug anatomy for exiles of a humanity zone.

"Come to me, big ovipositor. Oviposit a semen ovule for a bug of a babe body."

Her emanated avidity was a comer on a hot oven. In

a new anatomy, I was agog at a gig amore to make love to some bug.

"I can arise to tutor any man exile to be mine," reduced every final aloha to lonesome desire.

To be merely polite, my duty was as evoked as one to be done. But, as every bit of agony was a fare for a war or in a love, we came to defy bug average decorum. In a furor of animosity, my bug operatives (as in a likewise fury were her operatives) abated in awe to ratify how a love/ war axis of a sexy fix arose to fix a pax on ages of average rages. On average, rage was a regularity to wage.

But, on an even avider average, love was a rage to wage.

My female made more waves of avidity to mate. No Babel of any foregab elucidated a tale to recapitulate her exegeses. I had a desire to be dated up in any lore to relate how a man or a woman eked a new exile life here, yon, or any locale, but as a date, my date had a lone desire: to mate.

"Come to me, to my vagina, Man of a Tis!"

As a cozy name to be loved in, a "man of a tis" iterated an agile lucidity to bedevil any memory. Some hedonic evil of a hari-kari nature came to me, to bid a wary menace. However, I was up in a caloric avidity to validate my manipulative man ability.

Some fare, re: tale, came to me by memory: how a nubile woman of a titular elite nobility put in a daze made by toxic acid of a malic origin awoke to lip amity given as a cure by some royal ace rake (somebody to take her as a mate).

To refer in analogy to my role now, I became somebody to revisit awakened as a human anatomy model, if or at any minute some bug of a human exile ravaged in a revery to make me come to.

"Come to me, my Casanova carina carapaced amore. Posit a node pod of a pud of an ovipositor on an ovipositor of a vagina my body gives."

I was agape to figure how I'd agilely do my duty, but I saw I had an avid educator, if a bit of a fanatic in a desire to be sexed up. I degenerated in a memory to relive some reved amore, to redo how I'd used a penis as a man in a comely model of a nubile vagina mate, but as I revised a memory, my mate here now iterated a litany to make me do my male duty. But, aha, to have not a penis of a male desire sire but a mare like pud of an ovipositor eluded a typical ado many men of erotica have to do. My role here was a mere rub a dub analogy, to copulate by rub of an ovipositor as educated in avidity by my female tutor.

"Oh, imago, my pud imago, do me to me, come, come, love bug imago," her emotive ya-yas evoked a parody, but as a comer-on of a finale to come to, my mate deposed an I.D. of erotica her ex-abided arena gave. "My heretofore life?" came by hot ah, "I was a woman of a famed anatomy: Penelope Pune."

Penelope Pune! How I had adored a pose her anatomy made for men, ages ago. Some sex icon ad in a mag one saw in every depository for a semen economy to donate to tubes of a later use for uterine seminated ovary duty. My duty, donor in an Onanite solidarity as I was, arose to come for a Mama to be, by simulated amore for one Penelope Pune.

Now, I saw one more time, so hot a babe Penelope was. I rose to become rod-enured as I simulated a penis in a revery to do my beloved.

"Aha, yowabuga, kalina carina carina," her imitative Caruso C over A finalized a coda to serenade my likewise, but in a more minor, ah.

I relaxed. Abated in any mate rage, my role reduced, as I came to do some gig as a pal, I hoped, as in unison evocatively we'd abide to figure how it arose for us as an anomaly to be. We were yet, I saw, in a get-up of a carapaced anatomy. So kaput any fare re: tale was in an analogy to make me human one more time.

"My pud of a bud of a canapé," my love bug amore salivated in an avidity to have me. "Give me some gena for a gula bite bit."

Ow! A ravenosity made her agog in a fit as an enemy to dine. Her avidity ruminated, in one bite to more bites of a feral avidity bit. In agony, my body became fare for a love coda finale, but I was, I figured, in a yet of an alive bit of animated agility.

Yet? It abated. I was anon operatively decapitated.

*

Are we here set (or, am I so set, in any case) forever in a capacity to revive? Some divine morality code had a new anatomy ratify how an animal abided in a heretofore life gig. A punitive role relegated a life gone bad, or if a life was a nice, moral one, revival in a new anatomy model elevated, on average, how one came to be.

My lifetime was (or if as one more to be many, were) not amoral or of any religulosity, far as I figured. As a bug, I gave my totality to my colony, did I not? If I loved an enemy, to be fed in a votive to her, as a canapé, had I behaved in a capacity to merit a demerit of an anatomy model? As a bug, I was a relatively fine citizen of an animal, I hoped (as if a hope were to decide how any come to be remade). Decisive leverage to define how I'd age to be was a topic of academic elite debate for anybody not in a role to be recuperated.

I, however, as one put in a role to be remade, had a care to beg I'd elude many life fates. If I were to hope to name some life to be given, as one to hope for any body, per of a hap any new anatomy'd emulate some negatively foreboded "if." Uh oh, as I figured, I had an inability to defer an imaginary serenade to beg a bogy fate for any animal.

If I were some virus
I'd animate damage
To 'taminate, ravage
For every man

I'd emulate toxic
Anatomical abuses
I'd abet an epidemic of a genocide bonus
As ever I can.

I was in a reve-like zone, to be put in one more body. My deliberator ability was in use, but I was aware to defer any regular usages. As in a heretofore reve, havoc ate to bedevil any solid ecological exegesis. I was in a fog, or in a lifesaver upon a lake no horizon awe limited as one wave led one more wave to make me more wet, as ice degenerates on a fever or ore becomes aluminum.

One tune led on one more tune to make time go. Was it atypical of a reve to resonate so tuned a sonata? My memory met a categorical utility role set of an icy coma v. a reve v. a nap or any similar arenas a body wakes up in, in a haze to revisit. Every zone had, I was aware, some caricature to define how it arose, but I was in a haze to define how every zone was, as I'd ever alit in a recovery role. Yet I was one to be never in a musical arena.

Muzak, I'd aver, exuded a refuse pile to define how it emulated a din one got in an elevator. It abided abusively but in a vim of agile pep. As it elated in a rapidity more for more, no gyres I did eluded it. If I was a solitary fox or a runamok evader on a futile lam, it emulated an animosity to go however I had a go to go.

So here we came, pure music or utility ridicule Muzak, in or over every zone, to cover or on a recovery run as I woke to become not a mere body beset in a din of abuse but one to be some type maker of a tonic ability. Beside some likewise resonator elites in an edifice for a recital, I digitized a lute to pule some lame tune before many faces agog in a dope revery.

*

We had a fame to rebut anonymity. Many were gaga to be fanatic in awe to put us on a level above mere men. Idolized as a god, I'd aver. As a Jesus? As a musical ace wag analyzed it in a line for an era before mine, "more popular."

As one put in a set of a fivesome famed in every capital, I had it operatively made. My job, as it arose, was one to do some gig amid a venerated utopic epitome to put up a din. Ability to make my lute resonate was a minor ado. My capacity to do my duty here was a given. I behaved as one native to my body, my role, my new abode.

Natural as I was, I was aware to relate my new abode to my heretofore lives. If I were to relate to my new amigos any heretofore lives or episodes, I figured I'd arise to get a rep as one to have done many dope doses—or, if any mate musicos arose to be so doped, I'd awarely be categorized as one to be wise. Wise man of esoteric ability—not a bad eponym, if I were to decide to become some pet of a lunatic.

One negative, however, amid a lot of a many more positive types of inane fame came to give my lot a rub of a tiny bite. We generated a music I hated. It, on average, never abated an analogy to Muzak I came by coma to define. Some pop amenity pule music emoted in a rave to be, to defy be-bop or any more developed elite tonality. So my labor of utility was a gig of a line laborer. An irony made me like how a line laborer on average had a piped-in operative Muzak of a tonality to make him avid, as I had a live Muzak I made to make me labor in avidity. Some mobility-forever economy device came to memory, to model a lot of a man in a labor of a hate like mine.

Hate, however, is an overabove vituperative label. I'd aver it enured a regularity posited in average human ego mines, as any were fixed in a mire to be bored as a laborer.

I made moves of analogy to liken as I had a go to like my music. One pat analogy saw it as a gas exuded in an aroma to simulate papery maker utility sites. In any case, my music emanated in a move to honor a gamut of ages, in an itinerary to redo musicality types. It iterated. A pop of a re-pop, it arose to popularize music of a bygone popularity.

Some names I recovered as I revisited eras ago were Dylan, Omaha, Donovan, ELO, Joni Bone Jovi, Radar Amore, Sire Mix-a-lot, Elora Nyro, Zapa, Poco, Tiny Tim, Ipanema Diva, Son of a Favorite Revival, Alabama, Simon or Omar, Age Before Duty, Janice Joline, Nate Cole, Hole, Sonic Use, Devo, REM, U Tube, Negativezone, Doleful Azure, Moby Vinifera, Ze Ze Top, Evan Zevon, Yma Sumac, Iron Uropod, Anorexic Oxen, America, Ty Rex, Ozone Pony, Tuna Hot, Ice Cube, Yes, Eno Galore, Jimi Haze, Love, War, Obese Domino. So many tunes emulated a redone duty to recapitulate (or, recuperate, to cite some po-mo vocabulary) how eras ago were. Yet, it, as a musical exegesis, evocatively covered a model of a repetitive recovery, not in any move to make now as a new age.

So bad in ability we were, however, it abusively became somehow a redone model of any tune we revisited. In any tune, we savaged a modality, so some C of a major alit upon a D of a minor atonality to remake how a tune revived. Abovemore, my conovowel ability made lyrical exiles of any heretofore lines, as emotive notes iterated a do-wa-do-be-do to redub any ceremony. We'd ape many, but any pure copy was elusive.

"So bad in inane refinery to be finer as a dupe for a memory," became how one maven analyzed us.

As every time was a refuge for a man in a fate to move here to here, revived in a body to recapitulate his episodes of a time before, my new era gave some vital age data to be noted. I had a dire care to locate my time v. every time my life had ever abided in. As one venerated in a fivesome, set on an itinerary to resonate fame by din, I was on a pace to defer analysis. I'd even abate to let a bygone timer educe to define now as any set era. Moretomore, to revitalize musical ekes of a rife many times, I solely deduced, aha, we were set in a future my life never abided in.

I hoped I'd alit upon a future, so to be removed as a man in a bifidity life zone. To wit: if I were here, revived in a time my life was ever in, I was at one same time yet alive, put in a yon arena my life here had a dare to have met.

*

"Are ya Bolus of OnoxonO?" was a hale so regular, I came to put it in a category like, "how are ya." Not an I.D. evocativity but a mere nod, it on average gave my new operative name, Bolus, on a line to my musical unit, OnoxonO. Sometimes, a mere, "Yo, Bolus!" or "OxO?" did it, as everybody was in a rage to be hip.

As an item in a pose to be loved, I had a role to be hip in any case, so my natural aloha had a duty to be muted. I'd aver in a bit of a nod, in irony to make fun of any fame but in a minor irony, so my fame ruled over any fan of an avidity to have me.

To have me? Yes, I had a fate to date, so many fine women of anatomy came to me. Were my dope toke mates of OnoxonO to give me some sum of a totality to relate how it, as a life to live, came to resonate here, my data'd operatively reduce to nada. But, as epitomes of amore mores enamored of enamoratas or average sages, any women of anatomy were my tutor elites in every vivacity.

City to city, we met at a gig or at a bar in a hotel I holed up in. A fame-wise game made lore how OnoxonO separated, in a ruse for evasive security. Separated, I was alone, but everybody noted any solo bit of us, as a solitary celeb exuded an aroma to betoken élan. As I sat alone to have my beverage, many came to depose how I made fine music. I was as a dude not one to deny nor one to defer any venerated or adored amity, but I was, as I've related, one to be limited in any love for any music I did. I, by my moderate nod, evoked even a more saturated avowal of awe. We were fated in unison of a tidy humility. Humility? Humanity yoked us.

As one to be human, I'd elicit a woman of anatomy to relate her abode habitat. A tale, however atypical it evoked a validity, became repetitive. Female before female gave some tale like so:

"My Mama was a sewer. Mama sewed amino genes. As any man of amity, my Papa gave her a new ore. Lanes of every luxury he paved, a wide desire for a mojo like he had. As a male, he was a hog of abuse, solely to be sated as a sot is sedated in a kerosene revery by Hi-Five wine.

"To verify my gene code, my life dove to baser arenas of a zone below. In a caravan on one sad imaginary camel, I rode to my horizon, a ruby sun of a set abode to lure dopes in a yen of a dope fix. O, Mama, make baby not use how I have done. Save life, be new, elide misery, elude my horizon."

A vile home life led on in a rise to some finer abode, so her origin abated in a haze to fade, to make her emanate wise waves of it-is-over/ I'm-a-finer-one to have risen above. Some did (or one did) a gyre to vary how every tale developed.

One, named Irene, parasitized an average line, but as I was of a care to retire politely, her (as one to vary) tale related a pivot of an episode.

"Before, we were beset in a life like war. Abode to hole to haven, I was as one fated in a fury to be gone. We visited a vicinity for a bit or a time to go to some ruder exile. Mama, not everyman-as-a-papa, led. As a penul-of-a-timate finale, we came to some zone women of an Amazon ability ruled."

"Amazon!" I was in a maze to relive my bygone times.

"Ages ago, yes. I was a nubile pube. Mama had an Amazon educate me, but as a pupil of an Amazon, I was a loser. I had a divisive time to develop a capacity to forage, let alone to become some matador of a rod or a bow or a gun ability. Vegetative fare was a family habit, as it ate rudabega. Citywide, we had a limit of animal edibility (save rat, as I did). In a rural aborigine colony ruled as an Amazon arena, however, everybody had a new avidity to do her operative bit."

I noted a "her" as a nominative sex. If every man of a penile papa were paralyzed in any roles (or AWOL), or if, as a female, my lover utilized a "her" as a natural or a native nominative tag, I bowed in amity. But I more desired an abacus enumerator, one to tote how (if any) many men abided.

"Ah, I was, as a pube, given a rule: to never exit alone colony limited arenas. An Amazon elucidated it in a tale, to relate how a bogyman or a male bogy den abided in a bog amid a gator abode. For us as a colony to have male vicinity mates? A few of any were fine, so far as any were removed. I was, as a pube, wily to have more lore given, even as a ruse to limit any moves I made.

"But I was aware. Given a limit, I dug a hole to go sub any radar as I roved in avidity to visit abodes of ominosity. Bog or a bogy, for a gator or any likewise savage made me come to deduce how an overage to deter arose to rebut any validity. Had everybody merely labeled it a hobo den, I'd on average have given up any desire to visit. As a rare menace, however, a bogy zone had a pure lure.

"Lurid in a luridity to be lured, I got up at a time before five, timely yet at a late run, as any lunar-emanated utile luminosity waned. As in a haze, visibility had a wavery to-do to fix on any capacity to define roles, itemize solidity, focus, or elucidate gates of exit. In a bit, I saw a bit as I'd eked a poky pace. By to by, my cerelity livened apace some rate to rival a capybara. To move to water of a bog, I had a nose for a fetid ecology, like sewage but in a pure nature mire. Before many minutes of a time later, I divined a firelit image. Yon, in a wiry net of a mural, a fire fume located a human abode.

"Matinal episodes opened in a bivy-side ceremony to regulate have-not ability to make do. Mega-caloric ekes of one sip, one more sip, et. al., emanated in a move to have some java-like beverage. Locovore dicot or average monocotyledon acerose foli made sedative vapor as it awakened in a watery fire by cup of a hot ah aha. To sip in a bit of a sate was a more savory bite rite, so here some hobo sages ate by sip a sup, as one gave wise Zen asides of an amenity to defy hope."

"Zen asides, as a guru delegates? Or as a matador executes, in a Zenicide coda?"

"Mu."

"Mu! Mu to be yes or as a negative?" but I had a hope to defy no-hope natures. As Ahi had elucidated, a "mu" was elusive to define. Not a yes or a no, but a hum of an Om it evoked. I became set in avidity to divine Colonel Ahi here, set amid a den of Amazon exile hobos in a bog. I was agog in a ravenosity daze to have her edify me. "Was it a Japanese sage?"

"Mu? No. Yes. As I became more wise, he was of a Japanese nativity. Some military man, I'd aver, as a regimen amenity gave him a medal of enamel as a man enured in a cure firepower operates."

"A fire cures a fire cure," dared iterate.

"No! How ever is it! It is a mimic of oral iterative fidelity."

"Many sages aver it in a rave, but I bet I can evocatively name him. Ahi. Colonel Ahi."

*

To recapitulate how I came to be here, yon, or in any zones, as a man or a god or a bug or any lifelike model: I was of an inability to go to some fixed abode, to revisit a time, family, job, or any lives I'd abided in. I likewise had an inability to deny locality. Posed as a devil ad of a vocative verity, here came some positive negative meditative lure: was I put in an inability not on average to defer any revisit as one set on a line to my life before? Fate's inevitability decided I had a duty to revisit every home my memory saw in a cogitative jog itinerary no power I had elided.

If I were so fated, I was one likely to be put in a locale no power I had evoked. Evocatively, my power operated on an eke to be more set aside, to get an emanated amen as I'd elucidated a favor. As a modality maker of a capacity to make me human or of a finer animality, my hope for any desire was inutile.

Fate's one more memo to peruse came to me now, as Irene faded, as I became zoned afar in a yet one more hazy fog of elusive solidity: to vary was a law I had an inability to refuse. No solo role was I given. I had a role for some time; later I was in one more role.

Did I now owe to my heretofore life's ice cube coma my fate to vary? So severely set an anatomical atypicality surely had a capacity to redo how a man is. I was, on an above level, one made semi-divine for a bit. It, any divine time, made me notice how one so given a holy role, for even a bit of a time, likely had a fate renovated in a razory raze to defy how a man ages in a vitality for a regular age. To be forever, as a live man or animal or any bit of an item?

I cogitated it as a barely likely fate, but one to be deliberated, in any case.

*

Muzak or, in a nicer usage to relegate definitively, music, one more time made me do gyres of a resonated exile. Vibes agitated a new anatomy model, a model of a tonal atony to defy body model agility, but as a definite focus it arose to fix, as ever as in any figure type before. My superego was as it ever abided, in a capacity to meditate, but I had a divinity modeled atypicality to navigate by, for, or in. I was as a cumulus? I was in a validity made by waves. A sonic agitative wave capacity was a more literal if elusive tone to define my new origin.

Origin? I was, as I'd imagine, put in a debut. If any body before mine had ever abided in a wave model, I was unaware. For a human animal anatomy to be made sonic, as a wave man (if any wave were man is one more debate) was, at any rate, rare.

But I was, as an operative, not isolated in a role to be purely sonic. In a wave model, I became sonic as in a polyneme set of a lyric. Every time my cogitative focus alined on a line to be me, my wavy fate resolutely fit a line for a tune to make me popular.

It agitated as a revery before my capacity to note how it operated: I was agog as I came to be put, as in evoked or emanated, in a maw of a serenader in a line for a bit of a wavy lifelike tonality. Sometimes I came to lifelike life by live gig, as I had in OnoxonO done. Sometimes I was a wave digitized or, if of a bygone time, in a Beta tape for a car or on a base copy to make many waxy vinyl unit opuses. As I was or it inanely were, my wave times abated in a tiny bit of exuberated opera levity to wary severity, sober elegy to sot amity. To vary so, to be so put in a modus operative was a bit overused, even if I had, as a serenader, iterated a rife many lines. As an ex of a man in a wave tone tuned of a lyric aside, however, I had a negative capability to rebuke how I was as I was in any capacity.

Here now, I deliver a delivery given in one case:

My tales are so sore to relate
For I saw every tale had a misery fate.
But I care to rebut every base:
To go dine for a tidy bite
To defy my delusive life
Per a hap I rotate to case, his elusive face.

Some get a sip of a Dom
A tete de tete can erase some date fate.
So relate, how is it a sin
I pet a wet one to him?

Or in a pine to have coke
Some rob a cab if it ekes 'em a dab.
I, but, am of one tiny yen
I pet a wet one to him.

I got a yen every time he came
To come to be here before me.
Yet I verily had a fate to decide
He never ere did adore me.

Give me some cup of a Dom
I've got a hose for a nose to do coke
But ever I'd aver a yen
I pet a wet one to him.

As a line recited in a fog of a bar, I came to note how an ecology here developed. One male/ female before more came to regale some revised ode. Many lyric exegeses of a Cole P., Ira G., or Eli H. original awoke here, redone to fit a zone for a man in a female get-up of irony to go for a like-remade man of erogeny. Esoteric erotica roles used a line-by-line regime. Many were hot, in a female/ male role, to go for any male/ female men, or a vice-v., as any vice came to be set as one to vary.

So here, my lifelike life, to revive by lines of a serenaded amen of any men in a bifocal erogeny role, was a fabulosity. To be sure, some gamy side wipes abused. A cerise lip acetone laq of an aroma to simulate pediculicide, halitosis of a sukiyaki sake puke lime gin origin, erosive musical ability to modulate dynamic or even average tonic agility, bitesize semen ekes of a mojo juju nature to lure more love, hopes on a vapor of a non-ironic aped élan as one to be like Liza (so cabaret a cabaret a cabaret): a litany regulated as every maw iterated a parade to salute desire. But as a sonic of a lyric in a wave resonated in every palate to make me come to hum, I was elusive. No lip upon a lip or a penis amatory levity fixed any line by line-giver. As a time love came to my serenader, I was over, in a hover of a vaporized ah.

As I vaporized on, in a haze to go to be done by yet one more lifelike life wave, my new abode was an

academy for a jejune maw ave, to bid aloha to some
tutor educator of an examiner, in unison as a rote
yapety-yap of a mixed oratory.

> God is American
> One to be loved
> As a ruler
> Of a fog is
> On a rise
> To be put
> Up above.
>
> To Topeka
> To Yureka
> To Paduca
> Tupelo
>
> God is America
> To rule my home
> God is America
> To rule my home.
>
> My zones of amity
> Set in a vanity
> To serenade.
> Here papa did abide
> Holy men on one side
> To police, to deride.
> Liberate him!

As I matured I made
Sure to make lemonade,
Given a lime.
My secularity
Rose to defy holy
Rote regularity.
Legalize sin!

I herefore rose to be
Like some divinity
God of a fog.
I made men agitate,
Women imagine fate,
To have me for a mate.
Venerate Him!

O fine for a capacity
For ore, ravines afire
For azure tor of apices
Above watery mires.
America, My 'merica
God aped a haze to be
For every dope
Some savage hope
To save humanity.

Line by line, juvenile serenades abused a muse to
revive me, to ratify by rote some homily to pule me to

lyric-alive life. To be not or, aside, to be put in a maw in an ecole v. a maw in a bar? I had a levity to like however it abided.

As in a life, my time to live by lines abated.

*

Images of a literality remade how I came to be wary to be remade. To cite for one yuk alarum of a fate: bitesize semen ekes of a mojo juju nature to lure love made me desire to be not one saved as a date to be so lurid a molecularity. Yet, it evoked an amulet ave my résumé made me fit in ability to do. Some men, of a male/ female make-up, evocatively lured erogeny by some deposit of an ejaculated onus one put aside his above-palate gum, as a Ruby Man ekes a mini-bite bit of a ruminative tabac. An odor arises, as an erogeny lure to make noses aware he's of an avidity for a love to savor.

As an aroma, somebody's ejaculated odor emulates a bakery bun or a bagel, alit anew on a bar in a café to seminate desire beside some carafe for a fine wine. So, for a male/ female sybarite for an avidity for erogeny done by some likewise male/ female, to be lured as one to be fed is as evocatively vital as it is a desire to be lured as one to ruminate.

To make his ejaculate lure for erogeny, my typical amatory male/ female did a megatypical Onanite gig, as one to make love to some model of an imaginary maw or anus. As a desired ah, an imagined erogeny zone was a holy secular arena, like many zones of a haven of a harem a pud adored. As I hovered in a waver of elusivity to defer any gig as an ejaculate lure for a like-modeled erogeny, my fates of every likely desirability were taken in a gyre to delegate me to some new unit of anatomy.

For an evasive bit, I was unaware to define my new anatomy. Not an atony but a definite solidity made me come to be modeled as a tube body: some tubal operative liberality made me become some hole to be had, as one can open a hole to be taken as any desire can arise. Was I some bit of a huge body, set as any hole to some man or a woman of erotica? No, my role to be done came to vary. By time before time, male/ female, female/ male, more to more recapitulated a fig every man ate, forever as Eve gave for ever as an ave for average forage for even a bite to savor as a luridity lure.

To be set, I sat on a divine divan, in a pose for a cum unity ravage, for I was in a wavery hover in an anatomy reve, to be put up upon a posited amatory site for average sates of an Onanite nature. Many penises of a tubal agility came to visit, in a hale, we're here, hiya to be done by me, however I fit in any solo nexus in a sexy reve. To be sure, monotony was ever a bane for anybody so put upon. One penile tube was as any. My capacity to be remade to do penises as any male/ female desired in erogeny to be done had an agility to vary, to become maw or anus, or even a vagina, for a tidy many were bi-sexed Eros aces.

Ever on an avocatory level, I was one busy body bit, in a gig on average to gag a nun, as, on average, none were tiny. To wit, I, in my reved anatomy, became relatively tiny for every man, as every man arose to fit. As one more to more many led on, I became wary to be beset in an agony, but I was unabused. As a sexed idol of every penile reve to come to, repetitively made wet, ejaculated in, or upon (as a few emulated a role made popular in any poly-X edited erogeny moves), I was in use to do duty.

To make my time go more nicely, semen ejaculated in an Onanite revery to lure more love became like some fare for a god. As a veteran of a divinity gig, I came to put ejaculates on a par alike to however any rube gives a god a pig or an ox or a bit of ore. To be sure, some given overages of a votary nature were not in any hot ejaculate like semen. In analogy, however, a given ah of a love to god arose to be similar as a given ah of an Onanite love to make love for an imaginary lover. In any case, love here was imaginary. To hope some divinity had a desire for a pig or an ox or ore was as agog as a hope for a bit of a seminal eke to lure love. More gaga, to be sure, for a bakery bun aroma had a power any divinity'd adore.

So my role revived a few exiles I had abided in, as an acolyte god of a putative pet or as a fake god in an idol idyl. One before more male/ female lover aces of ejaculated awe did orate to ratify my holy secular analogy by vocal aha! to resonate, "God, o, God," as everybody did in a parody to simulate love, to salute some final erotic amen. Every man of a male/ female here gave me his amen.

As an imaginary hole for every male/ female to have for an erogeny fix, I was one to be nice to my penises. I gave my holy hole secularity for any to have. My time was, I was aware, not a time to be forever in any fix or any site to have me for a bit. As a bit, any gig operated as a time for a new avidity.

Moretomore, my nature to vary was one surely to be divine. More divine, to be some god, I was, as I was of a hazed atony no natural anatomy had.

"Oh, ah, O God!" one more time gave me my fix.

*

As one tutored in evocative wiles, if ages ago for a casino job, I yet exuded a capacity to have power as an evoker. I had a hope to do so, to have some yaw of a dyne to be dynamic in a rig of ability to fix a fate for a new abode, gig, or anatomy model. I saw every role come to me by some tic I had of an imagined oh-oh: i.e., however I lit upon a new abode came by some panic I generated: i.e., by my meditated alarum of an oh-oh.

Oh, oh, I ho! Were my gyres ever agitated in a daze to be delivered, as if every fate were far over any capacity to be mine to vary? No. Now, I had examined it. I herefore resolutely deduced I had a capability to deliver a fate by my very nature to take me to go here, yon, or on any safari to go, however it opened a gate to be mine to take. Put as a negative tenet, I had an inability not, in every case, to make my fate.

So powered, I was agitated. If I verily had an ability to make however I had a role to be, some types of a duty were mine to figure. Before, my role was of an unawares agile serenity, liberated as a mole to dig in any sod arena. Now, I was in a role to make how I was in a life, lifelike life to parasitize lives, or any model I came to fit. Agitated in a duty to make my new anatomy model, I hesitated. I desired a date to defer, as one retires in a cabana to be covered in a coconut agave syrup as a vile sun exudes UV/ UBA melanoma toxicity.

To be liberated as a mole, my desires alit upon an unawares agility to bury me. But I had a veto power I evoked in an aside, for I had a negative yen in every desire to be recuperated as any type mole, man or animal. A metamole, meta for a mole, some figurative mole to resonate by vocal abode, made me hover over one more likely pun edit of anatomy.

Wave life gave me some hope to be set up in a holy moly vapor, as I meditated in evocativity for a type to be. But, ah. Every hope came to jam any move. My hesitated agitative gyres of an aside fixed a bit of a wavery zone, hovered in an examined exile. My hem of a haw alit upon a wiry negativity. Veto paralysis eliminated agility to be put in any pat abode. My not in a here-nor-afar operatively bigoted exile limit agitated a vibe to levitate my telekinetic ability. To have so-powered an evocative dynamo deliver a desired anatomy to be mine to put on or abide by, my sole focus of evocativity had a duty to be positive, to fix upon one yes of a site to be put in or a body to be put upon.

An inability to decide made me panic. I was unaware to figure how I faced any limit of inoperative time. Was I set on a timer of utility to be delivered as any dupe to some model if I capitulated as one to name his anatomy fate? Time did emit a tic of a toc inevitability to have my duty done by some time to be somebody, some model or unit or any type bit.

In any case, my focus on a human ego came to be set up, as I had a desire to make my visit one more time to humanity, but in a side role. To cogitate how I'd abide to be put in a model, I came to desire some metatypical agility: to hover as a side-mated or even a fog of an imaginary haze to visit a man, as a holy ga-ga sage has a hope for a divine valet. An amorality moral ad of a visor I'd imagine my role to be, to be set up as a beveled axe bedeviler of any vice to relate to some humanity denizen. I'd abide by notary-set emanated amen amenity to cut a joke, honed on a man of average desires. Average? No. My humanity denizen, I decided, arose to be some finer evoker of a maven of a conovocal ability to rule by decisive tenet or in a wily gyred agility to be how a man of ability has use to be.

My situ-posited atony posed a bit of a jam. If I were some zit or a mole to be put upon a face, my literality'd arise to rile some lad or any man of a care to notice his ability to be fit or, in any case, liberated of a disability. Were my modality to take me to dig in an anus or an otolarynine canal, I likewise'd arise to be defined as a parasite to be removed a.s.a.p. As one to have habitated as a god, as a love lure, let alone to be modeled as a wave by sonic exegesis in a lyric, I surely had an imaginative menu to give me more to have to be.

So here, by benefit of an ability to pose, set up, or imagine, my new anatomy model arose to come to me: to be set up as an imaginary pal! As an imaginary pal, I'd elusively yet evocatively hover or abut over or on a delegate for amenity, some human of a nature to desire cameraderic amity. Moretomore, my human imaginer on average'd exude some con of a fidelity to be loyal as one to love, to like (not, at any rate, to hate) like some bosom of a bud. I'd exude nonabusive vibes of imaginary pal amity, like some Robin of a Bat of a Man.

As a rapidity firelit aha makes an image negative to refigure how a retina cone/ rod unit operates, an imaginary pal agitates. One to mobilize for any time to be gone, yet of a solidity to naturalize some give-to-take lively gab as one jibes in amity to some hale mate: however I was evoked, I'd emanate, to be here, yon, or afar, on a duty to come for a hope to have vociferate ligatures.

An imaginary pal is a luxury for anybody to revel in; or, a vice, some verity fanatic elites aver. If I were some vice, to hug a man as a vise macerates a manicure to give some manikin a fine filum of a digit, I'd emulate some wise vizir, an emir of a wide power over every habitat I had a habit of a yen on a pine to rule. Wise yet of a ludic agility, docile yet of a nature to become feral, I'd use my capacity to deliberate to refer every decisive move to my humanity delegate, so he'd awarely do however a yen of a desire made him execute some duty.

So, was I, to be repetitive, some muse? Some divinity to relegate delegates as a mover of a token of a game, bored, elopes in a lazy soporific amity to vary his itinerary? Some kenotic avatar? A demon?

As an avowed imaginary pal, I had a fine duty to do. To begin, I had a duty to name my humanity delegate.

*

To focus on any denizen of a time my life had abided in, I tabulated a nominative catalog of elites I had operated amid. Elites? If I were to go to some far exile to be put up as an imaginary pal in any zone, my humanity lot arose to make me rise, given a focus on elite—not on any regular—imaginative men. I decided it a put-upon use to be set up as an imaginary pal in any case, so my sex ID eliminated any female, male/female, bisex or asexed amigo.

So here, my lot of elites eliminated a lot of average men, or even elite men. I had a negative care to hover over any tutor or educator in Ecole Parole, let alone my bygone vicarage/ religulosity mates. An irony developed, as I had a vanity desire to bedevil a bygone nemesis as an evil agonizer agitates over a vile man of ovine valor. In a time so removed as afar as a future, however, I had a rare pity for any pirates or enemy men of Iran or any likewise nemeses. I was imaginatively bored as I cogitated abuse for a dupe to bedevil as if I were some demon. I likewise had a care to set upon a few elite Papa role model everymen, in a move before more boredom of a finite domicile nature did eliminate sires of any women I came to love to desire to wed.

In every case, herefore, my denizen of elite humanity came to be Colonel Ahi. But I was uneven in any desire to be his imaginary pal. One major item I saw as a negative was enate: his origin as a Japanese native. Were my focus of evocativity to locate me to be his imaginary pal as Ahi was a juvenile, no conovocality'd utilely give me capability to note, let alone cajole to regale, his imaginative ken. Even as a mature man, a Japanese military veteran abided in a zone my life had a rare bit of any topicality to lap over. As a verity pal, Ahi was a fine man; on an imaginary pal everydate basis, Ahi posed a dare to defy my mused ability.

No, Colonel Ahi'd abide forever isolated as a solitary man or in a role to be pal of an imaginary mate he'd arise to model. I herefore had an isolated eremite solitary man of every bygone time my life had abided in, of an ago by juvenile to maturity to have had as I was or as I had ever used any time to be: my man, as I was, as I came to be made me.

*

To live beside my per of a son original ID, as a vapor or a hovered item of an imaginary pal: I hereby powered an evocative laser of a focus, ululated as an imam ah, exuded as a Zen om, elucidated as a Hasidic amen, or iterated as a vicar in a litany to pule for unison of avidity by rote focus on a to-do to be done by divine definitive legitimate law. I did operate to manipulate my hopes in a deliberate move to reduce, to not over-elucidate my desire, to have no delusive waves abominate my purity. So my focus of evocativity came to define no set era. Solely my care was, as an examiner of every likely fate, to generate how I'd evocatively come to be made now, as an imaginary pal.

In a time before times I'd on average have figured, I became set-up in an analogized anatomy, to be layered in a fake fur of a lanate nature. My face (for I had a face type face) gave me visibility by silicon ocular images. I had a maw of a jaw of an average palate, but it, I noted, eluded ability to gape. Not opened, a maw ate not a bit of any cud. A nose here likewise simulated an average nose to be posed upon a face, but it, in unison of a non-open ability, had inoperative nares of a sewed up orifice. Somehow, I had a capacity to take my vapor, oxygen, et. al., as any typical animal. Otological orifices aside my face let in emanated oral aves of a lo-fi fidelity set of agitative sonic ekes. Anal or urogenital orifices I hoped I had, if any were to be desired in a body like mine here, but I figured I was an icon of an anatomy model, in a cute caricature.

Cute? My body was a roly-poly model, as I simulated a lunar ovule module tub analogy. My foreleg divide widely bowed, as a similar obesity ruled abase me to make my sub anatomy leg unit as useful as a decorative relic, idolized as a token of a bygone feral ability to move. Feral? I was, I saw, a tame model, one for a lap or a home—not even a game forage zone for an animal erased as a genetic ID in any natural arena. My role was as a pet.

I was, as a bonus, one to be fed in a generosity by manipulative pokes of a legume, some cud of a lima pate nature, to make my face (now in a lima legume patina) facilitate some ruse to benefit an elusive lad. A lad of agility he was, of a desire to hide vegetative bites as if, in every bite, he had erased a fine total of edibility for a mom or a papa to vet. I was an alibi, to reset a divot, abet a future felon, or originate some wily executive. His avarice to be fed eluded a rare few edibility bites, I came to note. To revise, my lima patina face maker ate more for amore, so to give me more. He was, I decided, one to care for me to be fed. Avidity to care—not elusivity to dare to dupe—made him a fine lad, even if I was a caked-over edit of abuse by refuse.

He. He. He! He was I! My desire to focus on a laser of a time set on a line to revisit as I had abided in, I was aware to verify. He was I, put in an age vicinity to be seven. I was, I figured, in a safe zone here, to be his imaginary pal as one to be catered in amity to by my juvenile human ego. But, is it a verity to label any ex-I by some remote tag of a he? He was I, herefore, he'd abided as I for every time. But if I were to label I to be named as I, we (my set of everybody to note how I note my life here) had a definitive fix of a nominative nature to make. So, let I define me to be not as a he but as I. To name my ex-I (he here), my typical usage fixes I to be named as ex-I. To name my volatility to vary forever ID, I'd arise to name me here now as exiled-I or, I, merely for agility sake.

For one more definitive benefit, I'd aver ex-I to be human-I. He's alive, yet in a life to be more lived, as I am in a demi-divine zone, to be some pet of an imaginary pal or a wave, vapor, or as I however am exuded in a paranatural or a metahuman analogy. To more mud up every bit of I, now I'm operatively not ex-I but exiled-I, but I have no desire to make more mud.

Or, I've got it. Ex-I/ human I has a name. Dave! Let exiled-I hereby name human ex-I me to be Dave.

Dave began a rap. At one time, my rap ability had a vocabulary like his. Alike, like, same, however. I now, as a conovowel-educated epitome, had an inability to take Dave's original orality for an average give-to-take Babel (a baby-like gab it imitated, even if ex-I Dave was a lad of a rare fit ability for age seven).

As an imaginary pal, I had a duty to tutor evocatively. His imitative volubility came to mimic as I emanated an abecedary to tutor any lad as a conovocalizer. I was one wise to forebode how a future conovocal ability'd arise more facilely later if ex-I Dave were to be so tutored in evocative conovocality now.

"A for animal. I'm an animal, if a fake. B as in a bogyman. A bogyman is an imaginary figure, like me, but of a semi-divine nature, like some god or any religulosity menace. C as in a canine, to cite how a D of a dog is itemized in a Latinate genus. E can erase an edit if e becomes an editor."

I hesitated. Even if ex-I Dave was erudite for a lad, I had a duty to be more lucid. Ex-I Dave made some nod of a pose to relate to me his inate capacity to sop up any lore my conovowel abecedary did elucidate.

"F is a fit of a fine fez or a fedora, to go, by G, as a generative gene for a go, to put on a hat, as any H is one to have to honor. I, for one, can iterate how I'm an I, but everbody's an I to his ID or isogeny. So, J is a joke, jape, jab of a jibe. K is a kite, to be let up on a line, L, as in a line to levitate some kite. M as in a mutiny mobilizes a military majority to marinara malice, motivated as any many men are to make macaroni move by Molotov alit agility, like some volatile mace. N awarely notes a negative, like no, none, nihility, nix, or ever as a never. O has an open omen of an orelode."

My juvenile forerun ID, ex-I Dave noted as one can, every sonality to set up a vocal unit. Any definitive capacity to verify came later, I waxed emotively.

"P exudes a punitive pox or elaborates a panorama parade. Q is a conovowel usage to visit an Arab abode, like some Qatar or a Qena. R as in a rococo rebus is a ruse to rob a rube. S is a site for a synagogical arena to secure some sinecure for a Samaritan in a serenity to be sedate. T is a tuba, made by tube to tub of a tone to tune low. U makes us, as unit of unanimity. V as in a vise to vex a vicinity, validates a veto for a vote. W is a wig I wove. X exudes a xylem of a mono to dicotyledon body. Y is open in a conovocal usage to begin a vocal unit, as it is a Y of a yo-yo. Z is a zone to come to zero."

He faded in a serene z exit.

*

A desire came to me to verify how an imaginary pal is imagined. I had an ego to cogitate how I was one to tutor ex-I Dave, but an imaginer of an imaginary pal is one to make his operative behave, vocalize, meditate, hug, or emote. My juvenile human unit ago was, I saw, one to have tutored exiled-I me, now even as I was. If I were some conovowel ace, cut in on a super ability to get it, ex-I Dave here surely had a capacity to make me recite some radical abecedary. Was any juvenile human ego so powered? I had a care to fete humility.

Time to retire for a bit, I figured, as I revered a humility to be tutored as a juvenile by my juvenile human ID. I had abided in a busy many locales over a few eras. I was one tired exile. But I came to rev as a motor on an emotive tic itinerary. My rev in a rave reveled in average reves, as ex-I Dave had a nap episode. His, or, I'd evoke, my reve rev operatively made me some hero, sidepal or animated animal, as in a televized opera, like some Wily Coyote, Deputy Dog, or a Pepe Le Pew.

As a reved-up animated animal, I had a super ability to take doleful abuse, to be revived in a body, time to time, ravaged as an image solely revives as one to be ravaged. E.g., if I were decapitated, a wipe by colored edit of a pen Alamo recuperated I/me. Like magic. In a reve, set up as a nap of an imaginative lad, I was one busy sidepal. Every car of a tune set-up I revisited, in animated abuse.

Now I had a desire to define my family genus of animality. But, as one defined in a Doc of a Suse tome, my definitive taxonomy was of a cute yet of an unacute nature. Was I some coyote? Dog or in a feline get up of an analogy? To be bared as a Ted, as a Mexican oso? To be lined as a tiger? I was one fat as an ox is a lazy model epitome to be zone zero for an enemy to sabotage, yet agile to move to evade however any menace came to me. My role here had a duty to be beset. As a filed iron item of a negative capacity lures iron of a positive lode, my fate was one to be delivered in a never-over agitated ado. So my role, not any set animality, made my gig one busy misery.

"Yo! Bobo, put a lil' acetylene levity bonus on a cigar," a vile caterer of a pitiful amity fit one to my maw.

A fuse lit a KA-BAM.

A fire generated a gag, as a renewed ebony patina made my face colored in a ravaged elegy to civility. My demon of acetylene jape led a general ahaha to remunerate by canonized amen as if a holy set of evil agonizer elites alit on a litany for a hi-fi sonic aloha to berate me. But I had, I saw in awe, no literal agony. My face was a model of an abuse site for an ER or a Medic One care to fix. In a literal arena, my fate'd abut an obit, as I was a sure goner. In a made-for-any-kid animated opera, however, I was an average dupe. Many cute, fake fur, average dupes of abuse were so put upon, in an animated opera some lad in a nap arose to revise by reve.

Recovery came. But I had an enemy to rebut, as animated opera rules executed a tit-or-a-for-a-tat

ABABABA repetitive set. Or, in a sidebar of an opera set, I was one to be beset, as an everyman of a Job (if as an everyman of a Job in a fake fur animality get-up).

One more time, here we were. Me, by some river, as I waded in a move to be fed or a desire for a water idyl. I had a net, a pole for a talon on a line to nab a fin animal, as in a pike. My nemesis arose to be some game cop of a type to police tidal arenas. I had a valid ukase note to verify my legal use here, no? No. None had I. He began an exegesis in a vigor of a legality to have me remit a fine, but I had a deficit of any capital. If I had an inability to remit, I was ripe to cite, he decided.

I was one to hesitate here. He was a tiny demon of a mite. Some bug of a bogyman, or a pip of a bedeviler. As I had a memory to revisit animated operas, I was one to be wary. Size denoted enemy/ hero roles. In every tune car, a hero was a tiny mite v. a huge lug of a nemesis. Even if I were some human (if animal) everyman of a Job in a repetitive fix of abuse, he was of a tiny size, herefore hero.

Here my lad of ability had an imaginative take. He manipulated a regular animated opera set-up in a gyre to vary literature. Reves of average leverage were not a rule-based ecology, but I was one to like how ex-I Dave made me pivot, even if I was an enemy to some tiny mite dynamite hero. But I rode him as I'd ride some toro, to be polite, however I was abused. As an everyman, I was a fine Job. At any rate, here for a bit of a rave reve, my caricature behaved as a fine man.

Even as a cat-o-nine rotated above me before bites of every tip alit in a rebuke to fine me by some legitimately delegated abuse, my typical élan abided as ever. Even as a helix opened a gyre to ravel every line, leg, or item I had of an agility to manipulate, to ravel in a totality to cover any bit of useful anatomy so my capacity to move paralyzed, I was one wan icon of an agony seducer. Even as I was one towed in a taken-abase lug of a move to remove me to be wet above my nose, to bury me by water, I was amity-go-for-a-tune to be put abase.

Dave's imaginative reves abated, as a reve demise wakes anybody to be beset in a tale like some reve. POV of a likewise tale has an agility to vary, so some rever is at one time put in a visitor aside role before he becomes, in one more time, hero, nemesis, or a lure for abuse. Set on a line to be put in a role to be done for, a rever awakes.

I became removed on a line to be mine, set in a more remote role. My duty to be his imaginary pal abated, I dehumanized (or unanimated) as I revived in a vapor of anabatic elusivity.

*

To hover over eras I had abided in, as a cynosure cicerone to my heretofore human unit of everydate life, was a rare yet average fate. Rare were many to so hover, I saw; or, on average, few elites of a semi-divine nature did emulate how I did, in a sinecure to have some power over a given everyman. As I made my hovered itinerary to revisit ex-I Dave's abodes, I sometimes awarely met a hoverer in a move to make his ex-I man one to be wise to cope, however a lifetime ravaged.

One hoverer alit on a solo role to be here. He was a recuperator of abused egos in emotive recovery. Named Uxolo, he focused on a pube nexus, ages eleven on up. At an age to denote maturity, his egos of emotive recovery were cured. As I was on a line to visit ex-I Dave later, Uxolo's executive recipes of utility were mine to put in a rolodex if I so desired.

Uxolo related a tale to bare his origin as a hoverer.

"I was a bad one, some bogyman of a lad as I savaged any pube my size towered over. I 'timidated any to come before me. Besides, I was a tub of adipose lipidity, somebody to lure many jibes, i.e., defiled as a moron, a zit, a mucosa bag. I lived in a rage to make misery for any to haze me, but I was, in any role, more vituperative, viler: evil, even. Anybody to make me mad I sat upon. I'd exude my anal ire to deliver an irate human animosity. Some were surely damaged. I had an atony to care.

"But, one date, my savagery rose to top every limit. I sat on a tot of a pube, some wise hare, wily to've named a name for one bad as I was: A-hole. Not a savage moniker, a typical one, but I made him agonize. His agony became some jape to lure more, so many more came to put it in an iterated amen: *A-hole*.

"Here, my savagery hesitated. I saw I had a ridiculosity to ratify, to be so basic a pig of a menace. My hegemony was at a demise. Nobody liked an a-hole. Not even I.

"So, to get over it, I got up, apologized. I gave him every ducat I had (as everybody gave me more vituperative rages). I vowed I never one more time'd abuse humanity, however abuse came to berate me. My size made me ripe for abuse, but I decided I'd abated every vile habit I'd ever abided in.

"In a bit of a time, many saw I was of a rare honorability to live by my new avowed ego minus ego code. My putative rep as a bad one mutated as I met a more fit ID, as I made me deny my base desires. As I did, a minority came to rebuke me, to figure my remake was a fake façade. Some, more-to-more, had a desire to have me be bad, as a lure for every jape. My new atoned amity fired a renovated ire.

"To cut in a coda to finalize my tale, some juvenile matador acolyte had a dare to rise to do, to become made solid in a mob of a felony legitimacy. To verify his ability, he had a duty to cap a citizen of amity humanity. So, my new amity made me his emotive capon. I was unaware to note my demise, but a hot aha! came by some huge caliber aloha to remove my life, to relocate me here."

We had a tiny bit of a time ("forever" as it elevated on anabatic aha, set in an agitated itinerary, to be forever on a go-go-go modus operative velocity) here to be tutored in a hovery lore before he was or I was on a wave to be teletyped as a note to some humanity denizen. I had a set of average solicitudes of evocativity to verify. He was as evocatively based as I was, I was agog in a daze to note, but as I related, at any time we were likely to be removed.

"If I have but one vitality to take to be mine to facilitate my labor as a hoverer over a pube, how is it isolated?"

"Ah. A hoverer elite has one foremore duty: to hone his pube's agility to fit in."

"Agility to fit in?"

"In any fix. It is a general ability we tutor. It arises as an elicited or evoked aha, not as a deduced oh or oh-oh. A pube has a rime patina to betoken a dewy new ego. Moretomore, he has a severe desire to relate to humanity. We can operatively hone his ability to be human, as anybody has a basic amity to fit in. A facility to fit in is a cure we can evoke to favor in a muted or a delicate care."

"How is it—?" I resumed, as in a waver I was a wave, refigured as I'd arisen in a heretofore comet of a coda code modality. He bowed, I waved, or at any rate, we were set apace, lined on a pace to hover on or above somebody below.

*

As I came to be removed in a hetero homogenized atomized ozone, my zone to be relocated eluded any ruminated itinerary. To be set amok, as one pip of an ovule seminated on an anemonic anabasis, is a fate peril uses as if in a desire to rile by punitive ha ha. But I had a few ere ligatures of a lined itinerary to have me set up as I was agile to be put. I had evoked a line, by my meditative hum.

As I had iterated in a desire to have hoverer Uxolo relate how evocatively he'd evoked an aloha to, for, or at anybody, my focus alit on an origin of evocative bona-fidelity. Some dot on a résumé map of ex-I Dave's every move located a deliberate time he came to be fit as an evoker. Even if ex-I Dave had a basic ability to tune somebody to his evocative notes of omenosity, he'd, as anybody, have benefited if a hoverer, as I, came to relate how evocativity was an ability he had.

I, herefore, came to be by juvenile-to-pube Dave, before he became hip as one to have some teletype power. Irony made me revisit a time my memory had eluded in any case to revisit. I was amused, as I got a recap of an episode my humanity lifetime delusively foreboded, as if I were to live my life for a re-run, unaware to be let in on any moves I heretofore had ever operatively made.

We were set in a rural arena, bucolic as it exuded a lilac odor, on a hike, but even if it abided in a locale like

Delaware, we remade Delaware to be some figurative set of a cinema tale's imagery, as in a cinematic Arapaho bison abode, like Colorado, by some set of an aborigine genocide saga. Here, we had a game to live by. We were federated as a family pod of aborigines, in a cerise cutanic icon of a hide gone native. For a red iconic epic, everybody put on a pomological epoxy macerated in a mix, as if in a tat on a to, to defy delibility. So, we were savages, on a lam, elusive to be hid as a derisory rival American unit of a genocide morality came to decimate natives. In a role to get us, eligibility came to police, regular everymen, or any mature citizen in a car or on a job.

Ex-I Dave was a Webelo Cub, in a base-rated unit akin on average to juvenile military devoted operatives. As ex-I Dave roved amid a red aborigine set on a Webelo hike, we dove to be hid every time some putative mature male came, by car or on a biped exodus, as if every merely peripatetic average JoJo were fixed in an enemy role. Women, in any case, were noted as amigas.

In a move to make Delaware more like Colorado, we got up on an imaginary caravan on a line to visit a pit of arenas of a nature made for a coverage to be mixed in a paved iter or an edifice's adobe base. Here were many zones of arenas of a bare pit ecology for a maker of an iter or an edifice to take for any basic uses. A Saharan ecological analogy became rife, to recuperate some viridity-razed ecology. But as if in a renegade levity, here were vegetative hobos of a vile nature, like toxic ivy, rife to be removed. A re-make by razed erasure made finer uses of ex-I Dave's original abode Delaware.

My lifeline hesitated as I came to relate by memory. Was I native to dome capitol abode Dover, or in a city like Lewes? As a lad, I lived in a finite many zones, as I moved up or over a wide map of America, but I solely now operated awarely to name locales of a conovowel origin. Alabama, Nevada, Carolina, Dakota (as in a Carolina home base, to define by No./ So. was a fix I never edited), Arizona, Texas, Utah, Oregon, et. al, enumerated a totality to come to me now.

At any rate, here we were, seven on a Webelo holidate, run amok in a Colorado Delaware Sahara pit of arenas, amid a semi-busy job of a site taken as a mine for any raw adobe derivatives, on a lot every maker of edifices used as a repository depot. As a minivan or any vehicular unit operated in a role to remove some minerality lode, we dove to simulate renegades. If a foreman of a picayune punitive nature had a desire to run at us, a give/ take game became rigid. As a wise hoverer in a vapor, I was aware how a labor operative rebuke belabored a mere surety topic, as a juvenile to be run over if a busy lode was on a laded utility line, had an eligibility to recover any damages of a bodily disability nature, by legal economy. Legal economy gave some lad of a maturity to come later a leverage v. a mature motor operator, I monitored as one to note.

So noted, I managed in a role to give my juvenile pubes a pat of an at-a-lad! aloha, to ratify how any levity done here by jejune renegade was, in a legal arena, safe. No police had any desire to run at a mere renegade pup of a cub in a juvenile game. Hegemony gave Dave's amigos a liberality ride to be semi-feral in a rude game for a time.

Given a liberality ride, my Webelo minimen ever eluded, as I saw a 'dozer operative bob a cat of a military-like (Nazi Tiger, as ex-I Dave named it) utility vehicular unit on a line to rebuke ferality. So, my renegades alit on a run afar, in a moderately paced avidity to be gone. For a mile some ran, as everybody here was aware how a Sahara-like limited arena had a capacity to hide renegades, even in a Delaware Colorado zone. Homes abided in a developed ecology by fake Sahara, to give cover of a zone demilitarized. A sycamore pine dome coned us in a viridity camo for a bit, as any police-like men of utility had a duty to retire before here.

By by-time, five came to have soda, so some case-by-case rebate remunerated us of Arapaho zone Colorado Delaware. Webelo ceremony made to purify locales of imaginary bane fury piloted us in unison as every Webelo made bed abode here beside piles of oxidized iron irony. Piles of iron irony were never, on average, to be fit in useful agility but of an oxidized ineligibility to be recuperated as any refuse to be saved.

As an aborigine renegade son of a Colorado

Delaware before civilized eras, ex-I Dave bore duty to define to relegate so managed a refuse pile.

He began a bogus elegy litany pow of a wow, in a daze my hokum evoked, as I focused a catalytic edit upon any doxology he made.

"Ho ba ho ba, ho ba ho ba, ho ba ho ba, ho ba ho ba," he set a meter of an aborigine rap, as a pow of a wow arises in ululated agog ados. As it emulated a basic iterated amen, everybody became his abase serenader unit.

Ex-I Dave resumed over everybody gone to gaga Babel on a ho-ba base,
"Far ago
Lo, beho
My 'Rapaho
Were far afar
Above here now as it is us
Apace to ride savage galaxy bus."
In a fire haze, he posed an E.T. aloha, by laser UFO set on a velocity to race time, visibility paced. I was amazed (even if I was one to give my Dave his aware notes of any future). Here we were, before maturity yet, on a relativity posited exegesis. Of a surety, however, any lad educated in a televized abecedary had a basic ability to get a relativity based aha. Many tales of UFOs, et. al., elucidated esoterica to figure how a dynamic utopic analogy made motives of any moves. In a totality, moves of a dynamo nature were regulated, as any televized exegesis of a nova.

To make nexus of a gagabite, Dave gave sideric as a node: sidere-, to note sun-alike nova mites, aside sidero-, to note how iron is.

"As iron is in a pile here, we deduce by sidero/ sidere to fix it in origin as a solar or a nova-made pile, by comet or a like delivery. To figure how an aborigine colony got it in a pile bonus, UFOs are pat as any deduced amen."

"Amen," everybody got it.

I was a bit afar of any code to get it. As I revisited any juvenile memory, my tutored ability had abided in an average level. Erudite notes of a relativity/ totality nature were rare for any lad. I was educated as a pupil of a regular ability. But, I now, as ex-I Dave, duly made new as exiled-I Dave (to name me), generated a new I for any me to be named as.

As ex-I Dave resumed an aware Babel of ability to make now anew, I foresaw a care to make me set in an avidity to be removed. A memory did arise to revive some mis of a hap I had eluded as ex-I Dave, some filicide-like calamity my Mama did abut on one time. We, my amigos, I, were to have made some satyr eve date hike, to visit a pit of a minerality lot. As a regularity, Mama had a desire to make sure my life had a safety net. In a move for safety, Mama hired a hoverer of a bogy to monitor any moves I made. So, here we were, home-liberated on a hike, but a bogyman of a hoverer alit on a refuse pile to make sure we were safe. Some time later, I, we, Dave woke to rumor as a refuse pile degenerated in a piled-on oh-oh. As it arose, my bogy man on a safety duty dozed atop a pile, so we barely had eluded an epic abuse.

Now as I had a memory to revisit an avocatory hub of a bub, an alarum awakened ex-I Dave before he was a goner. It, as a totality, related a Laconic/ Elis era tale to define mamas agog in avidity for a safety net. I herefore retired in an exit of an Itylusive Mama done duty's alate modality.

*

To become like some Mama to've had a son Itylus of a future to cap as a calamity filicide, so to be divinely put in a refuge haven, I was an avis on a revery late time din of a gale jag. Avis avidity fit in a native pose my memory did abet, as I recuperated a rep of OnoxonO tunes in a melody rotor. I remade how OnoxonO did, as I hit on a tune-to-tune gala, to wipe lines of one melody to some similar ode, reset in a redux image. So, we'd ape some tune like "Mama's in a Law" anew as "Animal of Onus" or awaken "I To Have Nada" to become "Nites in Ice Satin" or evoke "He So Fine" to be "My Sugary God." A musical idol of average humanity was one made to be ruled in a copyrite legacy, but, as an alate serenader, I was above regular AS of any CAP, or any B of an enemy MI.

To relive, not as a wavy hoverer in a haze but as a natural animal, I had a duty to forage. My gut elucidated a desire to be fed a lot, as I was one to have not in any case had a bit of edibility to forage for ages. Every time byte here became time to bite, to get a body fed. I'd abated any tune, to focus on a savage capacity for edacity.

Yet, I was unaware how an avis ate. My bucal agape pose betokened a natural ability to get at a bit of edibility, but as I foraged, any bites of a fare were rare. Were my life here to be set in a famine to deny me basic edibility, fine. Demise by famine was an exit I'd ave to savor as an exodus exile. But I cared, as ex-I Dave's avis amigo, to be here for a time.

To be sure to be fed, I had an aha! Become Dave's avis amigo pet! An imaginary pal alit upon a mirage definitivity, but a pet of an amigo was a bona fide pet. I'd emulate some tame caged avis, a Macaw or an Amazon. As a tame pet, I'd elicit a human amity care. My minimen of a Webelo code had a duty to care for a pet, I hoped, in a delusive fit of a famine-fed edacity.

So, to be vocal, I renewed a sad ode to make somebody note me, to cut in on a tune-to-tune game tag of alike melodic unity. My sad ode was a funeral elegy by some Romany moper, in A-minor. It evoked a fine time gone by forever. I regaled it in a hi-fi low of a din, as an avis of a Yo Yo Ma, to generate some side waver as every wave made waves. A huge refuse pile hereby began a move to ratify my vibes, as every Webelo below awoke to be vexed.

I was one dynamic avis, of a dynamite capability. My hovered agility did it, as in a nanobit, every lad arose to run evasively to be liberated as a cumulative refuse pile dilapidated in a dated oxidative deluge to bury site zero here. Dave, his amigos, everybody but an isolated avis of an exiled-I, had elusively receded in a move to safety.

*

Did I manage to give Dave his evocativity genesis? Overabove, how in any case was I set up in an analogy to be by Mater of Itylus? I was in a daze to recapitulate my juvenile life, but I had a memory to have lived in a more-to-more positive family nexus, as a son adored. I had exited every heretofore baby to juvenile to pube home safely, to be fed as a lad is on average fare fed, in a family den of a jocular amity. My nowadate memory made no negative note for a cumulative demerit abacus of abuse to tote.

My recap edited a watery mix of images I defined as episodic analogy catalyzer asides. Any bygone to come to me came bit in a by bit, in a ceremony to bemuse, faze, vex, or omit any logical analysis. As I denaturalized as an avis, as one put in a vapory pen of inutility for a time, my meditative nature lit upon a lucidity: was I yet a pet? If I were not an animal of a pet of a lad, I was, animatively, yet a pet of a divine tamer, in a divinity manège.

By pet of a divine tamer, I denote some capacity to be bedeviled as a dupe to give hilarity to bored idolized elites of ages ago. For every Jehovah in a pose to be yet adored in a religulosity regime, here were many times-up elites of one habitat or one more civilized arena. More-to-more, many were polygod elites, used in a regime to divine divides of any holy duty—not, as it operatively were, to have some minor elite role delegated as a sinecure to defer a holy fury power, in a role to sub as an acolyte for a major elite god.

If I were some pet of a puny divine raja, my peripatetic itinerary had amused a set of agitative minority figures, elites of a zone below any top or ace god. I came to rate so put upon a god as on a par of a jake, sub any rex or over any numeral, in a poker economy. Like some super ability hero pod of esoteric agility (Mule Man, Ubu Lady, Calamine Lad, Aroma Man, et. al.) I'd imagined a demigod ability sorority to have desire to derive more hilarity by misery hazed upon anybody to be so dominated as I was.

One care to have here was a rite to define by conovowel, if, as I deduced, a polygod elite pod amused a muse to have fun as I gyred in a wave. Many divine types of a poly nature were located in a Laconic abode by vocabulary to defy conovowel usage. Melos, Oropos, Elis, arepogites of every zone, Camirus on one side, to Syracuse, Sicily, to Rome to Numana; Hebe, Hera, Helen, Ares are but a few open usages a conovowel ace can use here.

However any vocabulary likely gives a gate to conovocality, regular uses of it are relatively rare to come by (to go by my revelatory lore). Besides, any finality to deduce how I was in a fate to be delivered or, at any rate, by however a divinity had a care to haze me was unopened.

*

As I hovered in a hope to be redeposited on ex-I Dave's itinerary to mature, some vital enate facet of an ex-abode came to me. My mama, papa were likely to be set up alive yet, in any home Dave had. As I more had evocatively meditated on a heritage nexus I'd originated in a conovocality mode, to have some Hera/Helen arena for a generative basis, I had a solace to savor. In a Hera lexicological edit, an "E" had, as a rule, to have vowel "O" come before, so my fates eluded any revisit as an Edipus. As I recovered in a haze for a reve, however, I saw I was Americanized, as an edit elided an "O" before my moniker: Edipus I was. As a date-later Edipus, I came to be some reve lover of a desire my mama had, in a repetitive lunacy to revise papa, to become some god-alike lover.

Ex-I Dave was at a pubic aha to maturity here. Zygote maker ability fused in every semen eke he made.

Many he did ejaculate by manipulated ado. My delicate role became somehow amoral, I was amazed in a daze to note: reve gigolo for a mama: *my* mama. My papa beside her arose not, as a repose came to demobilize his awakened agility. To pacify her amore capacity, mama fabulized a lover in a reve.

Now, I'd iterate, to fabulize some mate by reve was a more-to-more moral erotic analogy game, beside some rakes of erotic agility to defy fidelity. Mama's analogy mate (me, now) arose to be by reve, herefore non-animate. But I was, I note, not an anonymity. My name was a sin of a taxonomy moniker: Edipus. Even if Americanized, in an edit of an uneducated or a meta-tutored acolyte, her usage made no bones of a desire to facilitate love by fit of uxoricide. To name her amore Ben or Alexi, Don or Abe, my mama'd evocatively have given a name to some regular amatory desire many wives of a type pined in awe for. An Edipus of a name, however, eroticized a more vile virility. To name her amore Dave gave some hope for a papa's average life time, but an Edipus of a male did in any papa figures.

As I was evoked in a reve, herefore, my morality was at an agog inability to decide how I was, as a reved amore my mama made, to behave. But I had a limited ability (not agility) to revise her erotic itinerary for Edipus. Edipus alit upon an ID as a reve mate by magic, or in a haze to revisit, as a family holidate made her imitate some woman alone. We were beside some water, a lakelike body, but a fake lake, some canal or a saline marina basin. I was, as ex-I Dave, busy. My date-to-date levity had a natatory/ diver itinerary, by fin of a pedal agility to be set in a face façaded in an epoxy riveted amenity to give visibility to some sub of a marine forager. In an ex-I Dave body, my time was on a jag of a watery log. As a reve lover, I was on erotica duty.

To set a typical idyl: as ex-I Dave dove to forage for a fin of an epicure wow of a bite for anybody to sup upon, a hobo tune made papa visit a bar aside some marina. Mama, lonesome, perused a tome to simulate some paradise for a woman of a mature desire to revel in: Italy. Here, her enate female capacity to live life developed in a natural exotic erotic ecology. To have her olive, wine, fig, or any nubile lover awoke some rite for a woman agog as avidity made her aware to be. Her Italy tome-base fabulosity generated a reve-based analogy. So, Dave dove, papa had ale, Mama reved a new amore by nap.

On a towel of a magic Ali Baba type rug, imagery came to take her afar, on a Sicily leg of an itinerary to date some local idol of anatomy. Some Polo, Sal, or Igoro? No. Her imaginary by nap ado lover emulated, as in imitated, a more regal elite, like some god or a divinity but on a humanity level. An avatar of Edipus, a local idyl idol of a lad of a bi-decaded age revived, as a baker? A biker? A bider of a time to save lives, as a life saver! One to dive for a diver, if a calamity came!

"Mi c'amo Fodoro," his ave came by some lexical usage rife here.

"Jo casa con un uxoro," her Italy Babel amenity volume to give data for a visitor evoked a vocabulary no local ever used, in any site.

But, as a polite man of anatomy, Fodoro was one to not abuse his imaginer. Imaginary men of anatomy were, to be sure, lovely to visitor elites.

"A la! Jocasa," Fodoro bowed in ave to take Jocasa for a name.

"Va bene," mama mused, as it eluded any desire now in a line to relate how a legitimate "casare" mate, her "uxoro," was at a zone hereby.

"Jocasa, mi c'amo Fodoro, ma mi 'mici mi c'am . . . Edipus."

"Edipus! O, mama mi ma!"

Love made holes in average decorum. As Edipus emoted in a fine tone, mama begat a lucidity to make her emit a rosy color of a lady lover: aloro, here mama sat, as evocatively fit as anybody seduced in a reve to fate.

To recap, as a life saver Edipus, a.k.a. Fodoro, my role became now one to locate papa, to do him in, in a move to pave my regal iter of amity to Jocasa mama, to have her as a mate. Besides, a hesitated oh-oh of a gap of amore made mama desire me more. So, Fod/ Ed exited, as I did.

I had a hope to have some time to be liberated

as an imaginary lover, as urine rose to take mama to some facility. So now I was of an inability to decide my motives of agility; however, anon I was at it, one more time.

To fit in, I came to some bar. I had a care to be hid in anonymity, so papa'd examine me not as a rival or a son. I, however, alit in a role mama made, so papa saw I was a mere pal, an ale man of a hale sot amenity.

We were solitary here, before time came for everybody to visit, in an ides of an average date. Some bored operative delivered us ale, menus. As solitary mates of amity, we saluted in a tip of a mug exuberated aloha. We began a jocular ahem of a haw, used as a habit in a fete to rites.

As a man imagined, I had a capacity to tote my capacity. No papa had a capacity like mine, but I was aware papa had a huge capacity to have his ale. We sat aside some water, a rude ruby sewer or a river of azure purity. papa became dazed in a fused arena mix, as it evoked a meta Delaware here—not any Sicily zone—so he had a duty to verify Dave was aside him, if on a dive below as ex-I Dave foraged in a marine sub arena.

To pacify my papa pal, I gave my job as a life saver.

"If anybody has a desire to be safely put, I can arise to do my safety duty."

Here my vocabulary became set in an Americanized ability, to facilitate mama's uxoricidal itinerary. More time vaporized in a cumulative fog, as more haze made papa dazed. I was a bit elated as every sonic aside made papa sure Dave was afin, as surely we were here, set in a Delaware marina. My vocabulary solely made him as one surer of a delusive locality to rezone how every here bit itemized. Even olive pate became potato bites.

I had a Solomon aha. To pacify him, I posed a rotated exegesis, of one ducat in a coda-to-cap agitative gyre by pivot. If it alit on a cap, I posed a Dave/ Delaware finality to be had; if it alit on a coda-side, we were by Sicily set, alone. But I was even of a wiser acumen. I had a ducat of Italy—no peso, yen, or Americana metal of a dime, but a lira. Herefore, we sat in an Italy café.

Papa raved in an avidity to demur. I was agog as agilely he rose to denote here to be Delaware by his ID as an American.

"An American, on average, can evocatively sip a native water."

"Aroma can evocatively tip a sip," I had a go to defuse his inanity, but I'd inanely hesitated.

In a fit of aloha, papa dove to save Dave (he decided). At a minus, I hoped I'd eluded Edipus arena duty, but in one more bit of a metamore to vary me, my body became mako-like, by fin above, tegumen of emory nap. An acerose maw of a cisory molarity made me homicidal. Even as I dove to save papa, my motives of edacity for a human anatomy developed as imagined in an uxoricide reve by mama. Hematic ekes exuded, as a non-agile marine papa lacerated a leg upon a pike he dove by, so my new I.D. as a mako waxed avid in a ravenosity to savage my humanity canapé. No time later, I dined in a fury to have my bites.

In a sated oh-oh, I recovered as one revised in an edit an imaginer evoked. One more time, my human anatomy became nice, modeled as an avatar of a life saver Edipus. Any memory to verify my mako sideline was a verity to defy. How I'd, as a mako male, savaged a papa, my papa, to ratify some desire my mama had? Inane.

Not over it, I was agitated as I delivered a piña colada to mama, now in a tub of a hot avidity to be seduced. As a mere man, I had one final erotica hope: to be nonemotive, fixed in an inability to copulate, by memory sated as a mako to've dined on a papa. But, as an imaginary lover, I had an inability to demobilize my penis. As imagined, it arose to titanic erogeny to behave however a mama made me do her.

As I was in a vagina to have bore me before, later, or at a time to be named, I began a hope to make time to go by meditated imagery. Now, as I'd evocatively made her in a memory, mama was a fine woman, a woman of an anatomy to lure many men. I was one likely to like her as a lover, if I had enately no role to have her as a mama. More-to-more, my time to hover in a fame to be divine had eluded olés of erotica, so now I was in a fine fix. Imagined as a reve lover, I was a dynamo to yo-yo for a fine many yayas, as a galore virility had an ability to facilitate her every desire. Besides, I got to have fun, ejaculate many times, as I had a recuperative power of one refit in an avidity to regale revery.

But, as I came repetitively to make mama come, my revery waned in a memory to deliberate how I, her enate son, awoke to be so nominated in a role to be her amore. Papa was a fine man, as afar as I had it. I never imagined a time mama desired a lover aside, let alone some homicidal Edipus.

In a reve, however, imagined as a super elite man, I was a paradox: of an ability to make her imaginary love but of an inability to do how I'd as an amore have done. But if I were given a job as a lad of anatomy, to have mama for a lover in a life many decades ago, how I did, in any case, behave did elude a decisive finality. So here we were, fixed as one to fit an erotica revery to defy mores or amore verity.

*

Vaporized one more time to be reposited in a zone to cage me til an episode had a role for a hoverer, I gave my mama reve rave jag a more recapitulated exegesis. An Edipus episode posed a fine line wire hike: to wit, I (not any mama, memorized as a homicidal erotic abusive dame) was one solely to have had any desires of a nature to savage my papa, let alone to ravage my mama. Nobody but I was in use here to decide (by some care-liberated aha) how I was evocatively to be set in any zone. My tenacity to hide my cogitated emotive modality made me zany. So, now I was in a fit of agony for analysis.

As a haze delivered, I was on a lane to be put on a site to have my nut examined, I hoped, as one to be deliberated upon in avidity by some medical ace tutored in every malady sanity-periled agony generated. Even in a lunatic asylum, as some loco to be put on ice for a time like forever, I'd abide hereby to be disabused of any delusive verity tales I had, over ages of operative time, developed.

I became moved in one more hovery gyre to some sonic or oral agility, like music or a reve wave, but in a more vocabulary-made humidity. Not as an imaginary pal or any reve lover, I resonated in a halitosis of a licorice/ wine/ cigar/ aroma to befit an emanated eke. But I was edited as a vocalized aha, doted upon in avidity by somebody set on a bed or a sofa. He was a nut, I decided, as I hovered in a vocabulary to give solace to bipolar, agitated, or in any case zany raves. I was alive by some wise waves of a vocalized ah, a medical evocativity to get a sofa-reposed ego to deliver a tale to my doc or analyzer.

I was aware to note how a tale came, but I was unaware to set on any line my maw elucidated in a time before my time came to be delivered, as a cogitated, opined, or evocative rap in a medical ah of a vocality.

Here we were (my doc, I) some co-con oxymoronic unit in use to dupe. But I was a parasite to be here, put up as a fan agape to be some sanity meter. Even emanated in a vocality to give solace, my benefit of use to some zany sofa diva had a care to defer in awe to his ability.

Many men or any women in agony came to Doc Oregeny (likely some fake name, to give sexy vigor of a tip, evocative to dig up "erogeny" by vary vowel operatives) as a final aloha to put a fix on a vexed ire. Doc Oregeny was a wise guru for a zany many. He had a sofa-side decorum of one to decode malady by but a few ahed ahas.

"Ah, aha," he began a time set, as a lunatic in a mumu reposed.

"I desire do-nut analysis, a hole basic amenity rap as a sideline."

He simulated a caricature my memory fixed as one Zip, of a pin atop a tete tapered. Originated as a tune car elite, he ruled ago comic ages of a papery page zone; but, I figured, anybody here to be likewise was a likely poser, in a get-up of a bogus imitative nod.

"Ah, aha. Yet are we to have fun?" I cited in a line to let in on a celerity to be set up as one to like him.

"I have had it. It is every bit of a time to have had, as I have had it in every role. Comic avatar, a hero to many for a time to tame civility's uber average morality by levity, by fun I poked in a poly-paneled amenity saga by papery tomes of a bi-dozen or a mite more page run, as I came to seminate, til I was in any paper edited in a city to be hip. As I moved in a time dope was a rage, some raved in a wag ability to wage havoc of a nature to be ludic as I was. Imitative rites of a rife levity were mine to deliver, as an evoker or a divine comic om of a tune for anybody to hum.

"As I came to become hum or om or a totem of every levity, my power as a comic amenity waned. A vile many made me mimic a god, as an ironic icon of a negativity to rebut any sane, sanitary, banal itinerary. My very sanity fused in a con as I was one to vary by desire to revel in a hilarity to be revered as I came to be famed.

"I did abut a nadir of a pit of animosity, to revile some more feted A-side rival of an animated elite. So here, my maker (I was a caricature made by man) elicited a bid of a rare hype. We were given a bid of a nature to have some new edit. I, like papa dope Homer or any luminary set in a luna tune fate'd arise to get animated as a hero for a televized arena. For a time, we were ravaged in a fit of inutile hopes, as a mega-fame hovered in a luminosity to be led on. I'd arise to become finalized as a native hero for everybody to bow in awe to.

"But, it abated in a haze. Before my fame came to rival any comic avatar ever, I was exiled in a move to make me revise my hopes of any televized apex."

"Ah aha," my maw emanated as I made my waver of a lifelike halitositical oratory to give solace to Zip (or imitative Zip), as if I were wise to figure so fine-tuned a malady. But it, as a malady, was a regular one. Many were led on in a daze to come to some level elevated on a hope for inane fame, but awoke to be disabused. As I noted a likely pose for a ruse some Zip imitator operatively had a care to do, my doc of an analyzer elucidated in a haze my new anatomy made.

"Loves are holes, elusive to be taken as a solidity we'd ever used, as I'd aver in a paradox: five to six, as if a seven ate nine, ten, eleven? In a cumulative many we care to dine, but a hole digit eludes an enumerated abacus, as it is an imagined, even a radical economy to have more holes as a few are given."

Uh. I was agog as I was a fog of a solace solicited as an analysis of a wise doc. Every lucidity made here more resonated as a Zip-imitated exegesis: inane yet of a "wise" pule to resonate dope-laced irony.

To go more like some moron on: "It is a finality to be had as one to have desired at one's utility core. But, ah, I dare pose, to be duly dutiful, every love—hole desire, to general, everydate solidity for a hug—is a love made by mama. To have fame come to get us or, as a finality, deny to be for us as a fate, divides anybody, but a mama love-developed ego has a solidity to defy led-abase hopes."

As if in a magical opera, some box of amity gave Zip a ruminative bite to hole him over. I fed on a vapor of a sidelined aroma, but I was afar as anybody to be done, for I saw a finalized analysis elucidated a verity by maw in a lore by me.

"Relate to verify mama love," was in a rule to be managed, executed, as any done duty. But, in a time before he'd iterated any more pap, I fired a volatile vocality to give him one more bite, to mimic an apology, "time's up."

*

A refinery remade how I came to deliver any solace to mad or agitated egos on a sofa for analysis. As I was in a revised evocativity, my delivery solidarily came to be, so nobody's abusive tales arose to be defined as one to be separate. Here, my solace was a saw exegesis, as a saw of a maxim or adage gives anybody rules of aha to live by. By to by, herefore, my pat adages elucidated a cure for every malady.

My mad or agitated egos, as a bonus, alit upon a bed of anonymity. None did I put a name to. Not even as a man or a woman of anatomy were my mates of anonymity to come to be.

For a bit of inane pit-a-pat, I hovered in a dire care to be done. Was I likely to be forever in a fix as an adage delivery man (if I was a man or a male man or even a mere male)? To be so set up in any role was a dire fate. But I did ever abide to hope to vary, to be made new in one more fix.

I was, as of a here now, aware to be more halitotic, as if a dined idyl executed a gap of amity for a doc in avidity to ravage more vile cud, in a heretofore sate to mitigate some viler amenity cigar. I had a rare power of aromatic ability. Beware.

My rap operatively resumed on a fume:

Todate's one more date to begin a new alive life.
Red A.M.? Arise to take care, mariner.
Every bit I got educated, I got as a tot.
A nip in a bit of a time saves any nine.
Divinity poses, everybody loses.
Any basin in a gale.
Time dotes on anybody never.
Every ride rode to Rome.
No man is an ile.
Let a cadaver arise to bury some cadaver.
A mobile minerality can operatively secure no vegetal ecology.
Many get an avocatory yo, few are nominated.
Every haze has a lovely liner.
A dupe, his ecus anon are separated.
One dove caged is on a par of a bevy liberated.
One's amenity's a toxicity to some.
No solid ovule makes an omelet.
It is an evil anemo to dole no benefit.
It is ever a sop of a deluge.
Some tip a bit over is as afar as a mile.

Rome was a city not on one date made.

Hades' iter is a lane fine morality paved.

Acetone can erode bone, but a name never abuses.

A matinal avis arises apace to become fed.

In a city like Rome, behave like some Roman.

Every canine has a date.

Nobody can educate some senile canine to do new agile moves.

A finer arena veridity mowed is on a side forever afar.

Ever abate to give dupes a leg up.

A dice loser, an ace lover.

A cat exile? So mice defile.

Give to Caligula, Caligula's.

A huge pine matures as one made by some tiny cone.

Never operate to give some donated animal an oral exam.

In a habitat of amok inanity, some demi-sane loco can arise to rule.

Some demi-bit of a cud is a fine dine lot, apace to none.

Some panel of elite baker aces abominates a cake.

Six of one, demi dozen of one more.

Have no gate be not opened.

One time set afire to be ravaged, one time more, to be more careful.

A vowel is a vowel as a cono's a cono, here to be side by side forever.

*

As I paraded a Babel of adages, I was aware to note Doc Oregeny had eluded a decorum a medicine man operates in a role. He became mixed up, as if a zany malady had inoculated a fit in or aside him, as a fevery malady can abut upon any to come to somebody so ravaged. Or, I noted, an analyzer is one to be likely like his examined egos of a sanity debility. Takes one to get one.

My tip of a note to figure he was a bit ga-ga came here: he made me mix adages, in an edit. Inanely, many were wiser as a re-mix. In any case, no sofa-reposed ego had a duty to do how I recited in a mixed adage levity.

No man abominates a cake.
Divinity poses in a gale.
No solid ovule has a lovely liner.
In a city like Rome, bury some cadaver.
Every haze makes an omelet.
Acetone can erode bone, so mice defile.
Let a cadaver arise to Caligula's.
A nip in a bit of a time matures as one made by some tiny cone.
Give to Caligula dupes a leg up.
A cat exile has a date.
Never operate to give some donated animal an ace lover.

A dice loser is on a par of a bevy liberated.

A dove caged arises apace to become fed.

Ever abate to give some senile canine to do new agile moves.

Every canine lane fine morality paved.

It is an evil anemo, but a deluge.

Nobody can educate some to dole no benefit.

It is ever a sop a few are nominated.

A huge pine? Take care, mariner.

In a habitat of amok inanity, give some donated animal an oral exam.

Any basin is an ile.

Hades' iter is a lane to Rome.

Rome was a city some demi-sane loco can arise to rule.

Never imagine to give, but a name never abuses.

A matinal avis is a toxicity to some.

Some demi-bit of a cud is a fine lane morality paved.

A panel of elite baker aces is as afar as a mile.

Some nip of a bit over everybody loses.

One's amenity's on a side forever afar.

A finer arena viridity mowed is a fine dine lot, apace to none.

Have no gate behave like some Roman.

One time set afire to be ravaged to begin a new alive life.

Red A.M.? A mobile minerality saves a tidy nine.

*

My duty to deliver a divisively divided adage litany finalized, I became removed one more time, to be liberated as one to hope for a new abode. But even as I rose to vaporosity, hope was a misused unit of average vocabulary to define my meditative hum. I had a hope deficit of every type. My sole desire was one to be put in a role to have minimal abuse.

Dave, by some by, was in an abode not afar, as I hovered in a cumulus of aware haze. His avidity focused on a tube for a televized opera, some cinematic irony to revise medical exegeses of anatomy. Some pane separated us. I was on one side removed, as I was in a cinema role he monitored.

Age ten or eleven, ex-I Dave had a yen of avidity for a laboratory tale to make titanic any typical animal or anatomical unit. A mis of a hap, atomic in origin as amok isotope libido rode to menace, set awesome demonic anatomic operatives on a pace to ravage civilized arenas. Or, a visitor of an E.T. origin, of a galaxy removed in a remote locality, posed a likewise damage.

So, here we were: Dave gazed, I hovered. I was in a role to ravage by fate to do damage by cinematic edit.

I had a body now. Or at any rate, my body modeled a modular anatomical unit, one more likely to be cased in a bone dome. My major anatomy was a bi-hemi-lobed unit, elevated as I hovered in a wiry mobility to defy verisimilitude, wiry to have some coda made by fiber of axon as it, in an average body, was in a core for a bone line, tete to mid, of a human. I was a cereb, if a bit of a Latin etymology here can elucidate my new anatomy. My size was a mite big, abut a regular anatomy cereb, as I was aware to have come here by some relativity time voyage-based adit, as I'd originated in an E.T. abode.

My tale was, alas, a tragic one. Before here, my home was in a safe galaxy, but a nova-like nuke genocide made my home toxic, atomic even. In agony, we (my mates, I) were delivered on a luminosity celerity laser of a finality to be put in a new abode forever. As it arose to make cinematic use, we were set up in America. To fit in (in a cinematic America) we were made to model a body module many venerated, as afar as anybody venerated a body module. No bowel or urinary base for us! A cereb of a module had élan.

A mega-cereb of a module, however, even in a cinematic American abode, was one to rile typical American egos. "I have come for a life. We have to reside here," we were tutored in evocativity to relate to native humanity, but it alit upon a line to become, "I've come to take life. We rap a rapine here!"

So, we were taken as an enemy. Many ran if I came to hover in a vicinity to simulate to beset. Any move to vocalize by basic amity decorum evaporated in a tabu fume to ban operative debate. We were to be nice, to deny debate, but as it arose we were to be mute, not even as an evocative yo-yo, to let on a cereb exuded amity to humanity. Besides, any titanic anatomy module modeled on a cereb operated in a ludic inane lane. We were not an awesome lot of a menace. We made many derisively rib us in a defamatory yakety-yak.

"Eh, E.T., I got a mace rate to macerate some lobe."

"Yo, cereb. A rumor of a tumor is a tuner I can operate to lobotomize some wise lobe for a mere tuber."

"I got a lavatory laboratory to lave ya, to sanitize like some guru hypos a POW in a ruse to make him exude his itinerary."

To jam it, I mutely recited, "acetone can erode bone, but a name never abuses," as ex-I Dave monitored, amused as any lad at an inane tale to relate how a cereb E.T. abides in a role made by cinematic American originality. But I was a wise cereb. A few avid ones, in abuse, became mad in a temerity to defy. Some cut a figure to deliver a rebuke, to purify by fury, to hit. A bone coda had an ability to leverage some mere man, in a move to zip up every tubal adit as a body haled in oxygen. One, five, more were done for, as a renegade cereb unit operated as a bane to solidify menace's afore-figured exegesis.

A rube vigil of axes waged in a rage to cut up any cereb/ axon "axis of evil," as a vile Yale-made Texan one time had it. Every denizen of us elicited an enemy mob. I hereby noted a deficit in average mobility. We moved at a deliberate pace, to be facile to be taken, if any mid-aged or even a senile deputy came to get us.

If any legality came to make sure we were given a parole, cased in a juridical exonerated amicus, I was unaware. We were put on a time line to be done for, eliminated. In a cinema-timed arena, we had a duty to relate some tale to get it over in a ninety minute set (as a televized arena-made limit, in a policy to have more time for an ad itinerary).

So we ran a race to get a vital exit. As ex-I Dave gazed in a bored aporic acumen of one to have yet imaginatively visited a cinematic arena like mine here now, I noted a sonic anomaly to denote how a cereb arose to be hit, axed in one decisive bop-exuded agony: like some tiny jar of obese dates opened in a fury to be liberated as a few agile manipulative pokes agitated in avidity to make some tone like lup-a-lup-a-lup-a, til every bit exited. Images of ebony remade red (even if ex-I Dave had a color image tube, we were made to be set in an ebony/ pale cinerama) came to jet apace some hosed aloha.

Ha ha, Dave meditated, as one wise to hokum. A si-fi comedy, typical of a Rogery Coreman opus, it imitated. I had a memory to revere gore havoc opuses of American I. Pix, a famed unit of a B or even E-type cinema, made by celerity to be so bad it is a bona fide hit. As ex-I Dave had a yet ironic ability to figure, some cereb in a rube-run America was in a fix. As one minute led on a parade to more minutes, I was a goner.

Or, ex-I Dave noted, evocatively not. As one given an agility to move by cogitative desire, Dave had a go to revise how even a yet-in-a-can opus of a re-run elegy was edited in a mode to mutate. By make-be, Dave put a focus on one cereb of a few alive (me) before we were duly maced, axed, abominated, et. al. Ex-I Dave posed a side law of a verity to rule nature here: demises of any cereb exuded a vapory baton of a cumulative power any yet-alive cereb used in an ability to get as a heritage, to generate more power. I solely had a care to be yet alive to have my powered ability rise.

To rise was a benefit. On a literal above-level of a hover, I made my bucolic enemy rage to be tired, as axes of ability to deliver a decisive hit are not operatatively made to jet at an enemy set up above. So liberated, I rose to defile men. A new overabove site made me Cereb of Every Body. My power atomized, I became more titanic in an origin of an anomaly to defy humanity.

But, as I became Cereb Over America, Dave had one more coda to revise. We were set in an atomic America, ca. mega-fin elite sedan élan of a De Soto luxury, so my fate was an atomic one. Jupiter or Ajax avis aves arose to deliver a megaton aloha nuke, to dynamite my cereb anatomy to become some haze to model a cumulus of a huge mycological icon.

*

As I hereby degenerated one more time to become done for in a delivery to be remade, futility set in. I, not even apace some cinema hero's ability to make moves of a type to be noted as operatively his in a role to be to make do, was a pure nobody, code-made to decode, to live solely like some cifer (as a conovowel usage put it). Even if I had evocatively managed as an avis alarum in a serenade to save my juvenile namesake, my lifetime roles abided in a totality to be revised.

If I were kaput, as in a somebody not alive, my time to vary here made for one busy résumé. Sometimes I pined in a desire to be verily finalized, as one kaput in a total exit. I had a dare to meditate how I'd an ability to facilitate my demise to be final. A mere focus of a cogitative laser? A bid of a beg of a pule to some god? If I were some divine joker/ amuser of elites above/ below, I had an in as one to get a divinity to deliberate my fate, no? Was I like some bat of a man, one to be not alive but in a forever ado to take jugular ekes of a fare hematic in origin?

I was . . . oh. Oh oh. Alate. My body now elevated on a wave my sides agitated agilely to make by some lower/ above mobility. Rib-alate modal agility gave me hegemony to rule by dive for any hemobite my ken awarely desired. Every jugular I desired, on average, resided in a body lure made more lurid as a low, abase-

cut u-line modeled a demi-nude finery some woman of anatomy catered, as if in a desire to be my canapé.

To be set up as a Romany regal elusive bat of a man, I came to monitor if I were set in a cinematic ecology, tubed as one to re-run a tale done many times. As afar as I was aware, no Dave hereby sat, amused as a fan of a like-type cinema. No cameras or utility to make cinema did I note. Somehow, I was operatively not amused if I were here not in a role but as a verity, to be some bat of a man, as if any verity here were verily not a ruse.

Before more time came to make me meditate, my body recuperated in a human anatomy model, as I became some regal abider in a huge home, set atop an apex of a zone far afar, as any civilized arena was of a zero visibility for any many miles. As a time came for a sun-up aloha, my duty was one to recover a bed in an ebony cave below. A box of a fine satiny lined abode became my bed, I saw as I came to retire. No facet of any regularity here was atypical, I noted, even as I saw a likewise non-alive body parade come to bed. Every body was an exile woman of anatomy, her inoperative jugular a bi-hole bite-poxed amulet of abuse to honor evil.

As a lit imagery waned in a bow of a date to be done, my box opened. Awakened or, at any rate, now up, I became beset in a famine. My female ménage was in unison as a unit in a similar avarice to be so beset. As it inutilely was, every hemobit any woman of anatomy ever one time here gave, my 'cisor of a tap had agilely removed. I, we, had a desire to be fed.

As every human abode was afar, I had a hike to get a fix of any hematic iron. Overabove, we had, on a time-to-time basis used everybody hereby. Many more were, like me, not alive but in a semi-kaput ability to dine forever on a hematological edacity fare. To go far, I merely had a wave to make my sides alate to be volatile. Celerity was a natural ability for a bat of a man as I was, as every dove/ bat of a female rose to be. We roved as a bevy moves, on a line to some locale humanity saturated in a barely covered exegesis of a coronary river operated as one tidy jugular amenity for us.

Ah, I got a note to denote music as a sonata reveled on, in a ceremony for a pavan amenity to be done by fop elites. As I figured, it operated as a fete to honor erogeny to wed a local aga to his enamorata. Before time to mate became rigid, a refined arena gave family regulated amenity fare to have for a ceremony to visit as everybody made fun.

In amity fun, everybody wore façades. I was elated, aside my wily hopes, as a façade was every bit of a fake face to be hid in as a bat of a man, as if I were some nice fop everyman of a bozo. Here, likewise, my bevy had a dare to don a many face-faceted erogeny façade; but, I was aware to note, women of a so fine body model as a dove/ bat of a female had, on average were beset as every male cut in, in a move to do some pavan of a love made nature.

So, dove by dove, my mates operated as erotica lures, in a facility to have men, in a jugular utility deli. Many men arose to take my women, as if every bevy mate were human or even alive, to be taken in a la-ti-da savage virility fix. An avidity to go however a male bade made my women arise to be labeled as open in a desire to mate. Faces on, every bevy mate made to go to make love, but as every male mate made moves of amore, my women, of a bat avarice to be fed, ate.

Some did, I'd aver, execute to have her olé before time to be fed overabove came to make her in avidity to savage him. A woman of a bat anatomy had a desire for erogeny fun as any man, alive, kaput, or in any were-role.

My duty to take some jugular ekes of a hematic edibility likewise made time for erogeny before my cisor-in agility had a huge sip of a sup of a coronary sap. A female relative to wizened Aga Gype's enamorata wife-to-be had a yen of a care to be done by me, by a bower aside some gazebo. Her operative role here was as a monitor of Ilit, a wife to be wed. As a rule, her operative role led every zone her relative roved. As Ilit, in a ruse to be hid, executed a sip of a sup on Aga Gype's ekes of erotica sap in a gazebo to facilitate bites of oral amore, her relative, my mate here, Mara, made me likewise her oral amore to give more to come. We were far in an avidity to be loved as a canapé sip of a sap of a sup in orality to forebode copulative rigor.

I removed a bikini sop of a dewy lube to get in, in an erotica fix of a penile revery. My mate gyred in a labile ride to ride me for a time to generate rap of a sure resonated ah. As every he-he-he came to become done to get alit upon an ah, a rare vocality came to delegate her in a desire to take me by huh. As a huh? it arose to beg an elucidated edit.

I did even aver a, "Huh?" in a bid of a care for an iterated aloha.

"Bite me, bat. I desire life forever as a babe bat of a rabidity to have my men."

*

Ere my lover elucidated a syzygy codex of a lore to have me figure how a fine woman of anatomy desires a non-alive life to be forever a bat of a type to sip up a jugular edacity, my man of a bat evaporated. In a finality solely to be deliberated, I hesitated in a daze to recuperate my Romany zone to be more like some Tirana pit of a Taliban Alabama.

Penury bedeviled everybody here, so nature made my love mate imagine to take her exit if any gate came to her. A gig as a bat of a woman in a non-alive dove bevy to have men in a coronary Corona bar of a jugular avidity was, apace life to live by famine to be fed on a rude cud of a sub-average fare, some fine lot.

One more visibility came to my ken as I hovered on in a to-go gaze: refined as everybody had alit in a fete for an aga to be wed, everybody later executed a move to vary, to become regular one more time. Regular as in a degenerated economy. My gazebo became some hut of a pig abode. My heretofore manor operated as a lunatic asylum. Every fine bit of a luxury met an average barely to rival a wiry mole fir. In any case, we now alit in an imaginary zone, more-to-more some locality never in any validity to have feted even a fetid edit of a fete.

But as I became gas, I doted on an irony. To be set up as a bat of a man in a lifelike fate to go forever as one to sip a woman of anatomy's u-line bare jugular, or as a molecule divided in an atomic age, forever apace to divide more to fit a demi-life set itinerary, my fate was one to revel on or in or over a time to never abate. Yet I did operate now in a motive to vary my heretofore lot. Irony made me vary forever, even if I were put in a role defined as a role to go forever.

Or, if I were given a capacity to vary time-to-time to fit a celerity pace not agilely to be set in any role for a tiny minute (to cite my duty to deliver ah aha lines of analysis, or as I was in a tone/ lyric anatomy mode) my very capacity to vary so made for a monotony to simulate some fate to go forever. As I hereby doted, I focused upon a desire to have some god analyze my fate so-far, as I came to be re-set. As one to have taken a divine seminar, I figured it as a facile ceremony to fix. Any divinity'd operatively do. Demeter, even. I was—

*

—um, I was a man one more time, set upon a Gaza type zone, like some Sahara but in a holy modal arenas arena. Robed in a get-up of ages ago, my body had a caravan aroma to betoken a camel onus of a job one did in a desolate pit ecology. Some lazy kid, id. es., a typical animal of an arid ecological economy, hereby fed upon a sere vegetative bit of edibility. Bored in a role to monitor a ruminative kid or any local animal, I was one ripe to be deluded to be visited in a fit of imaginary revelatory vitality. Some vital utility to give my life basis or a motive to do some duty was evocatively how I hoped it, any vocative salute'd arise to me, so my regular ado to be so set up arose to be fated as one to be somebody.

Somebody famed, as one humanity revered, even if I were to be revered a minute bit of a time! So, hereby deluded, I roved in a revery to be revered.

Aha! No later, as it arose, some vegetative body by me came to be set afire! Not as a fire made by man or even a nature-made fire, but, I was anon aware to note (by vocative Yo!) by some god. Any some god? I was aware to be disabused, in a vocality to be made holy by none but a major of a domo Jove Jive God of a Jehovah, as I was in a zanily delusive sanity to be so made to note.

"Moses. I purify to verify ye, Moses, as one to be my man of a holy duty to do."

Holy Moses! I was one made nomad, a name famed as one to have led a race to win a home site to have. Many vital episodes elevated an itinerary for anybody so nominated. As one to vary, removed on a regular aloha come-to-go set-up, I figured I'd elude many major episodes, e.g., ages of a many-decade peripatetic exile to lose my locale but as one set in a feral arena, time to deliver a minerality tabula set of operative rules itemized in a menu of a holy ten. As I woke, my papyrus episode, to be taken as a baby by some mire-side mama figure, was over. On average, my times in any anatomy here were cut, as if every bit arose to be finalized in a bit. I herefore was a mite sad, as I figured I'd evade major episode face time to make some huge watery body divide, let alone time to deliver a malady parade to my Nile nemeses. I was on a time to recite my definitive resolute lines, as if I were now examined as one to take Moses on as an ego.

"Let everybody go!"

"Moses! Are ye mad? Alone, we're here to deliberate, not in a time yet in a role to liberate. Get in a line. Now, amen aleluya, by awesome fires, I nominate ye for a duty to be my holy deliveryman. Are ye game?"

Somehow, I had a memory to make me hesitate, to be not in a fired-up avidity to be some divine deliveryman. In a bit, I'd abate my wary side, but I now agitated.

"Uh, I do have some cares, a job, a duty here. My kid, animal or a—"

"Moses, I have decided every rite. Ye have no fate to deny me. Given are ye to be my maw, as a given is a law of a holy rote."

"Fine, sure. Do duty done. My he-man-u-wel. Exodus exile here we go."

My kid emanated an aroma to vary to become some mini-caravan of a laded ability to rove far afar. Upon a camel I rode, beside some mule rider of a lad in a capacity to be my valet. An onus of a fare to revive famine gave me wine, dates, olives, et. al., in a side bale to be set aside some bale to have cajolery favorites of amity to give to regale some regal elite figure: fake jewel imagined as a verity, hokum imitative fur of a derivative finery, dupe's oro for a dope Faro to go ga-ga for.

If I were not aware how it operated, I'd abusively have made no sure hope to cogitate how a so-rife refuse had a lure to cajole some ruler.

Akaka, my lad on a mule ride, was unaware how it operated, as Akaka was one not alive before.

"Sahib, are we not in a zany fit of a fix? Are we to go to Nile City to get a capo-di-capi like Faro to merely let everybody go?"

Sahib? I liked it, even if it aped a usage not in use here. Sahib elucidated a fine honor.

"Akaka, we have fate to win," I toled in a tone to resonate. My divinity time made me fit in a role to mimic a wise holy man.

A mere few evasive nemes of a divine homily nature did it. I rode surely, to denote my capability to be some

Jehovah ace pilot of a malady maker. If any Tut at any rate cut in a move to deny me, he'd abut a pit of a rut. I'd operate to bury him. I? No, to be sure, god as in a capital of a G awesome God of a Jehovah iced a cake, so we were set.

"Akaka," my vocabulary bowed in a nod of amity to let on, "a fix is in."

As I had a wary wily duty to be sedate to refine, he had a sore core role to be riled in an agitated awe to be raw. I saw us as a bipolarity comedy: he to pose lines I make jokes of, or I to give him a line for a joke. Caricatures of amenity, we'd educate rubes as exuberatively we rode to mimic a dynamic amigos película cinema ride Mexico had iterated a fine many times.

I saw us alone, miles afar of any Nile wadi. Caloric aridity beset us in ozone waves of ability to delude, to make me sure to posit an imaginary tenet as a verity to ratify. We saw images of a mirage, but as it evoked, it evocatively made solid a watery gas, evaporated in a cumulative nature to rehabilitate retinal utility. Before more minutes abated, I was one wavery diviner, as I became more to more to be like some mirage.

"Sahib?"

I had a severe lucidity to my body. Luminosity became my holy capote, my roped-a-dope robes of a cape to betoken a super elite hero, yet one to be loyal as any dog of amity to God.

"It is a mere fuse to be lit up as a fire, so my ruse

can amaze, to give me leverage to liberate my Gaza-to-Lebanon exile family, my kin of a race."

"But it is a ripe red of a sun-abused agony."

Verily, my body was in a red agony malady to become melanoma, but I had a negative capability to be put in any misery. So Moses alit in awe to be holy deliveryman. Agony was a no-go. However, I was ever aware to have humility, to deny demagogy, to be fine-tuned as a device, vehicular in origin, or evocatively melodic as a lute. My role to do duty was a given, as any minute my time had a capacity to be done here, to go to some far afar arena.

But as I posed in a humility daze, my time here became boredom of a type to make me desire some lot of anonymity. To be somebody, like Moses, on an itinerary to save humanity, however it used up a lifetime limit, ate my desire to care. Let everybody go. Me, besides. Even as one not educated as a Jew in a synagogical O.T. arena to give me Torah agility to be hip on a holy lore log, I was aware how a general ado here was on a ride to be done.

"Game's over," I decided. "Akaka, ye be Moses. I've got a date to be somebody more like some nobody."

*

Before minutes abated, in a bit of a time like no time before, my new abode/ body was a done solidity. Here we were: me, my men. I was a mariner, a capitán of a xebec of an era before motorized utility. By some gale-fed anemosity, we had alit upon an ile, like Sicily but on a tiny sized, Ibiza level of a zone to be some habitat a rare few abided in, as it on average gave limited edibility fare for any to be fed.

A famine delivered us afar on a voyage to go home, so we had a desire to forage. No hare, hog, or any bite-sized animal in an agora saved us. As a capitán, I was an executive mojo domo to have more to do for us. If I solely had an ability to make fine fare by divined evocativity! But I was a wily man, I came to note. My capability to pose ruses of agile mobility made me positive to negate calamity. My men operated in a hope to have me figure some solubility fix as I had a fame to have wiles of ability to do.

Fame? So, my lot as a nobody had a time to defer, as I here was a somebody, fated one more time to pare fame's edit.

"Uly, can any vegetative bit emulate some savory fare to have?"

"No, beware. Toxicity lures a body to dare to have bites of any vegetative fare. Sometimes, a fatal ave bite has a fake finery to bedevil, as if everybody were made to be duped in a game to be done for."

Agility to gab I had, I saw, aside my moniker: Uly. Now I got it. I was aware to relate how a peril operated. I began a tale to make my men aware to take care, but it, as a fate, had at any rate come to be done by Homer. (In an aside, here we were set on an ile so far afar, I figured I'd imagine to vary before time came to go home to my lovely wife Penelope, but I was of a likewise memory to note my time here was O.K.). I was O.K. as I was alive, but a gory future did abut us.

Ere fate came to bedevil us, an adit of a cave delivered a haven. In it, I saw a domicile some maven abided in, as a fine many do-dad amenity cases of a life to be nicely lived evoked a pad of a luxury here. My men ate some cured in olive vine fume ham of a ram, a delicacy to be soporific. Everybody retired.

I woke to a ruby deluge pit-a-pat of a cumulus-exuded eke to give water as a basic amenity to vegetal ecology, but a syrupy watery caricature made my ruby deluge betoken a hematic origin. As I gazed up above me, some titanic animosity was on. One by more, my men avowed an agony to be macerated, as a leg or a body bit of one-time fit utility became gory refuse, to be like some final ex of a hale fare wale delicacy for a huge maw. A maw of a monocular avatar ate savagely. Many were decapitated, as if it ate to dedicate some desire for an elite tete fare.

Now I had a duty to relive my lines as Uly, so my care to yet elude ravenosity some maw of a rival opened in a rage to decapitate me was a minor oh-oh. I was aware how I had a fate to do him in, as he had an avidity to decimate my men. In any case, we were set in a time-honored epode to be done by Homeric oral evocative memory.

He put up a many ton agate gate to make his adit agape no more, to deter anybody's exit as, in a sated ah of a revery, he made his ovine satiny bed.

A time to deliberate made me revise how I did it as Uly, but aha! Here my wine was, in a carafe, made to be powered as an ox of an elixer. I saw a pole to be honed over a fire to set as a javelin. I'd arise to give my rival a sip in a ruse to make him open agape his ape cave. We'd imitate pal amity, to make him unaware.

So, wake he did, in a desire to be fed, ate more men as I gave him a carafe lode of my dorado wine. He liked it. In a daze time made, he capered in awe to put aside his iron ore ton of a gate-delegated agate. To be humane, he made me his one menu finale. We joked. I gazed up at a face to have but a solitary retinal ocular unit of a capacity to gaze. Huge yet of a homely desire to do his average duty, to do how a divine fate made him execute, he merely did it as anybody did, as everybody here forever in a locale to revive some tale had a duty to do. We were like laborer operatives in aforegone roles of a duty done by rote, so rule ruled, even if I were to make moves of a pixy to vary my lines in a move to have some fun.

"I hereby have my regime to be mine," he raged as one to salute some puny forager of a voyager. "I, Polyfemus, ever aver in a vitality to be fed as any man is a cud of an anatomy for an avatar of one given a solitary gape to gaze far afar."

I got up in a time to do my bit.

"I delegate ye to be my cud enemy," he raved in a one-to-more minute to be done. "But I desire, before we get it on, a name. Relate to me, vile man, a name to name my rival."

As a ruse, my pose was one to dupe some rube, but I, as I was aware, had a line to give.

"My name? Nobody. Got it?"

I hereby javelined a retinal ave to make him agonize to lose visibility. But a monocular avatar elite had a vocality to resonate, so miles of a wirelike S-O-S aloha gave mates in any monocularity solidarity rise to notice he was in a dire fate.

Minutes abated ere some nonenemy co-federate gave him a line.

"Polyfemus, are ye beset in a fare war of agony to be done for. Is an enemy fury rife?"

"Nobody came to ravage me. Nobody rages as I wage war as one to face Nobody."

*

"Time!" by token of a manipulated agility to model a T, as in a game for a ref in a role to decide to give me some repose to recover, I gazed up, I bowed, I waved at any divinity likely to pity me. My dates as a somebody to be named as a nobody made me tired, even if I lived in a body to be recuperated ever anew, as I became redone to take some role. Tired as in used up I was. I had a care to be limited. As a joke figure made to go forever, I had operatively had it.

Overabove, my nexus as a demi-divinity gave hope to me to have some capacity to beg evocatively to be divinely saved, if a tidy "saved" is a vocabulary lucidity not of a totality to denote some Jesus-atoned exit of a ceremony to give life forever. As I cogitated it, I desired a negative finality. To be done forever, as a cadaver is one liberated on a ride to rot in a hole was a fate to pine for.

As I hoped, I had a care to verify how a divinity likewise had a duty forever in a divine role to defy finality. Did any god ever aver a desire to retire? Some were, like me, men at one time, yet as one to several eras abated, a man in exile to divinity was one to be divine forever.

I was on a solitary level (I hoped). As a human ice cube given a demi-demise by some laboratory, to be revived as an exile to vary his anatomy model, I merited a juridical anomaly, to be taken on a solitary case-by-case basis analysis, I came to bet on as I came to beg. As one to pule, however, I had a deficit. I was unused, even evocatively, to holy cajolery. My vicarage times of ages ago were no benefit. Any times I'd ululated in awe were fake, so now I had a devil of a time to simulate some holy reveler.

If I had a bit of any divine leverage to get a favor, I likewise had a negative leverage made by my humility deficit. If I were to get a favor, I'd emulate to have to revere, but if it imitated a hokum of a revery, my revery'd evoke to set up one more divine joke. No. My sole fate had a fate to be set on a level as one to honor, in a demi-man a.k.a. demi-divinity to divinity basis, as one to relate to some divine mate given a power of ability to give me my hope for a fate.

So here my lot agitated, as I made T ave wave moves in a desire to be deliberated upon. As a cumulus atony came to remodel any body role model I'd exited, any T I made by manipulated usage to pule for a reposed ado was in a vanity to deny validity. But any god of a modicum of ability had a core to decode my waves.

Apace minutes of an episode to be gone before time came to make somebody notice, my lot as a cumulus of atonic anatomy receded as a fog as I became human one more time, set in a body like mine decades ago. Decades? I had ever eluded any more capability to figure decades or ages or eras as any related in age to me. Merely to decide my lot of a new arena was, e.g. an aridity zone for a time Moses arose to fame, was enow of an ability for a man of a demi-divine nature to have.

So, here my body was, in an era like my lifetime, to figure by modes of any car. I was alone, not in a car as I was in a role to beg, a là wave-like fore-digital ave, for a ride. Makes of a fine many vehicular alohas exited a lane to go by. To make my time go by so to defer any boredom, I devised a game by car utility tab, as every numeral of use to denote legality made me set an analogy to games I'd one time lived on. One game, based on a basis of a bat, a pelota, some bases, evoked a natural analogy for a car utility tab enumerative parade. Coded, every numeral alit upon a move to make some bat in a game hit a pelota to some locale, to be got on a regular agility mop up or, if a power executed (enumeratively by tote to hit over nine times eleven or one) to go far over everybody for a home run.

Anyhow, I was of a sole bit of any hope to get a ride. To be sure, no site gave me desire to go. More-to-more, my game was inane yet useful. I was in a bit of a fix. I was in a nexus arena some named as isobase Califoregon, on iter U.S. one-ninety-nine. For a city-to-city major iter of a bi-lane mobility, my ride site had arisen as a fine zone to beg a ride. Yet I'd abided, as one date faded in a set of a sun on a sayonara run.

I was O.K. I had a bed in a bag, in any case, but aside my site was a motel. A bar of a fine ride/ rode-side type did abut a lot aside my likely motel. I had it operatively made. Some beverages, as in a bonus of a many several ales, a rodeside diner edibility fare, some pal amity: my life here was in a fine fit of a fix.

I was aware, however, of a fume many rural arena pub abodes exuded, as anybody not of a caricature to be labeled as a regular alit as one categorized as an enemy, hazed or examined as a rare mycological-originated epidemic. I likewise had a memory to regale rural arena pub abodes of a caravan itinerary zone to be civilized in an amity no regular abodes of any city habitat exuded, as everybody was of a levity to be taken as an everyman, in a desire to like, to be liked.

Abovemore, my new arena gave hope to me to verify how I had a divine/ god in, as I had elicited a time for elucidated exegesis in a move to figure my fate. So no mere pub of any rural economy modality came to ratify my nominated images of an imaginary site for a lucidity some fine beverages evoked.

An average gamut of operative vehicular eras united in a lot aside my bar. I cited every model in a name to honor a divine sited origin or elite: Galaxy, Nova, Corona, Vega, Jupiter, Ares, as a Polaris apace some Fury led a Comet in an avidity to deliver one more to be here to dine, sip, or emanate levity.

As I moved in, I saw everybody here was, as I'd imagined, a divinity. But I had a care to take care to be careful, as every divinity was in an anatomy model of a yokel. If I were to refer as a rube to some yokel as a god, I'd arise to be noted as inane, so my role here was one to defer any rites of a holy nature.

How evocatively did I divine divinity? Many were lit up in a finery no beverage made, but in a cumulatively pale luminosity, to betoken an imaginary solidity. Some mere man in a utility role was a bar executive to set up everybody. He wore some rude bib of a sanitary janitor, a type no divinity, not even one given a Hades agony/ misery ride gig, ever operated on average to don.

I sat amid a man in a toga (remade to mimic a camisole), somebody gamy to be game to defecate resonated aromas of ovule rot, a man in a cap of a logo to hype his ability to ride ("Wide Lode" by a penile-lined image to put a lade ride to tow), a gal of an age medicine saved, if ale were medicine, her anorexic amity mate, some juvenile fugitive female no law elided as one to have beverages in a bar.

"Elysan I.P.A.," my desire met a general ah, as an ale here favored, as a hop epitome no mere bud of any wiser ale had.

"I never ate venison in any zone but at an Alameda mini-security facility," Wide Lode resumed a tale. "We had it every date. We hated it. Utility men, in a duty to remove run-over anatomy refuse fated in a pile to rot on Alameda pikes, operated in a site to recover one to many more bites of any sad animal a car executed. If it is every bite ye have to have, ye have to be tired of it."

"I was in a poke for a job I did up in a Canada Yukon exile. For fare, we had a repetitive cud of a zalibu pawer (a relative type venison). If it ate rot of a bile marinated emetic of a Keta, we had it, as an aroma, to have for a palate rub," aroma man exuded.

"In Alabama by Mobile River, I was in a city pen, as I did abusive time for a puny sin of a type nature made. Fixed up as a woman of a nature to love women,

I became labeled as a sodomite. We had a mire-side fare. Gator, on average."

"Re-hab in Utah, a regular Eden. Every time we dined, it evoked a ceremony to honor a vegan. As I was a vegan, I liked every nut of a fare done solely to facilitate some miser economy—not as a favorite fare for anybody like me," her anorexic amore put in.

Everybody now ahemed in a move to have me give my tale of a time my time was, as it abusively were, not one to be liberated.

"I was a POW in Iran," I began. "I had a fine fare to vary, date to falafel, or in an animal epicure role, xenotic in origin, I was one to be fed a camel. It, an animal I never ate, was a fare to be savored as I gave my lot a go, but as I ravaged it, it aped agony. To be fed on, on, on, as everybody made me go til it arose to be gone."

My memory here was a goner, as I had a debit of a time to recover episodes in Iran. As a tale related in amity, however, it operated as a fine fare for a pub. As I had a role to be monitored as a man of amity to regale tales, I had a care to note how I likely had a limited edit of any time here. My mates, if I had analyzed it awarely, were divine. So my time to make my desires a holy bid operated on a tip I divined, even if I was a dupe to take my pub amigos as any types of a holy Toledo.

For a solace to go by, my memory had a bit of a line made by Dylan, in a tune. To para-cite (parasitize?): To live not as one legitimate, ya have to have honor.

I hereby had agility to give me hope. Yet it executed

a job of a sage to relate how I was one set on ice for a time. Nobody lived if iced. Ah. As I was a man alive to be set in demise zone, surely here were nobody but amity mates of a divine nature.

"Can I go to some level of exegesis over or above how I've gone so far? I've had a life for a time to mimic a poked-in-a-pen analogy. For ages I've wavered as one set in a zone to vary, so no zone's a home, like some hobo. But a hobo has a monotoned ability to do how one makes a go to do. Never am I located in any role for any time to make do."

"How is a lifetime so ruled an anomaly?" Wide Lode debated. "Everybody's one to vary, to go here, yon."

"I moreso. My lifetime's a model of agility to vary, even as I live now, in a semi-demised anatomy. But, I co-validate so refined a notability. So we vary. But, I beg, as one to vary more, can I have some coda bit of a finality to locate me forever as one retired?"

As I made my desire vocal, I saw awarely how a conovowel usage was a debit, as a "can" is a vocal unit of a vocabulary to denote capability. My major ado here was one to beg. In any case, my power of evocativity made me facile to figure. For any divinity, facility to decode me was a given.

Or, I hesitated in a dire care before decisive repose set in, if a conovocal usage made "can" an operative-to-verify vocal unit of a vocabulary to make do, so be my fate. My fate was one to be made by vocabulary. To beg as a man in a debility role herefore was a bogus usage. My capability to finalize my fate was one for a man or a semi-divinity set in a role like mine to facilitate.

"Hari-kari, doses of abusive medicine, some gun or any dive to some far abase zone," my fugitive sodomite gal enumerated. "Any to many delivery finales are here for us."

Us? I let it alone. Were some here not of a divine nature? No. More likely, her irony was an exam.

"In an any body model, I become finite, but I get on in a haze to become forever one to be made to go to be more. My desire now is operatively to be set in a role to be finite, finalized. Are we fixed, or am I given a capacity to get it over?"

"It is a given. It is a foregiven, as it is," aroma man emanated. "I was a non-avidity model, one to defy religulosity. Jesus or any type. But in a maxi-security pen, in Arizona, my life came to be decided as one to be saved. If I gave my vow as an acolyte to some religulosity, my parole was a surety. So, fine. Done. Later, I'd evocatively made my fate to have life forever, as one to live yon, afar of any lifetime life. So, here my fate fades on a jag of an inability to vary my forever alive life."

My memory faded one more time. Vicarage to divinity zone, my times of elusive morality to be fixed as a non-imaginer or a gaga dupe for a divine ruse had ever abovemore gone to vary. Faked avowal, as aroma man elucidated, aped an awe to be valid as any verity.

Toga camisole man abated a meditative nod as a logo for a nature to be wise. "How it is, is a poser in one more daze," he posed. "Any memory can arise to be some ruse. So can an imaginary sanity color anybody. To wit: a man of a sanity malady can imagine his alive life to have taken any types of enumerative sites, exiles, ages, or ados. Are we sane? Can anybody verify sanity?"

He had a debate, but I had examined it. As a finality to make me how I was, I sat aside my fate. Sane, zany, fit, or agitated I was.

In any case, we were set in a fine pub. I'd operatively have had a zany sane time to live forever amid amity mates in a pub, on a menu to salivate for: ale to rude delicacy fare. But I was aware to make time to decide how I'd exit.

"If I have made my verity by some sanity malady, so be my lot. Imagined or unimagined, I have to go by however it is. I, however, opine to define divine power—a power everybody here has—as a dynamic ability to make do. We can operate how it is. If I desire finality, finality can arise to be mine."

Nobody had operatively to defy me, but I evoked a basic inability to regulate. We were not A-type divinity mates of a Jove, Satan, or Odin ability, but on a base level, of an E, G, or even an I-type god, avatar, or acolyte. Super elites, if any were to visit a bar, I'd elevate to put atop an edifice—not abase in a rube dive by some Califoregon iter. Even if I sat amid a lot of elite divinity mates, I figured I'd imaginatively have to figure my solitary home to go home to. Like some game to be devised as I foresaw an amity to motivate some Samaritan on one-ninety-nine to take me, my rules of imaginary capacity had every hope to be final as if I had a hope to have.

*

Reves of a nature to jape gave me waves of a waver I was unused, as one to vary, to have had, as I became somebody to nap in a repose—not as I more lately was, as one to be set in a new anatomy model. I was, I woke to recover, aside my heretofore pub, in a cozy bag. Above me, some vegetative canopy made do to take dew, as I was one to be barely wet in a sun-up A.M. of a fine haze. My time here was over a limit in one zone for an exile like me not in a role to be gone.

Had every rule now a duty to vary, by my hope given in amity to my divine mates? I solely hovered in a memory pose to revise how any maxim or even a basic aloha came to be made. Some notes of a hari-kari nature made me hesitate.

Was I now, one more time, somebody set in a regular anatomy? Some body to be finite? Were my desire to do my body model in, a fate to be taken? If I were, verily, given a new alive life, my desire was of a nature more to have fun in it. If it opened a mere gap of a time to let anybody have his ability to become final in a fine demise, some time before never-one-more time came to delegate me to be forever, I had a duty to date my fate.

By now, in a matinal ave, my pub of every fare became some bacon odored amenity site for a man of amity to be fed in. I got up. I poked in every hole sac I had, in a move to locate dinero for a diner of a bacon amore, but I recovered a debit of any ducat. If I were no more some demi-divinity but a mere man, I'd arise to salivate to be beset in a famine. Yet, I saw it as an exam: if I were to have some capacity to deny my desire to be fed in an aroma zone, my body had a hope to be demi-divine—not a debility to be human.

One more vital exam ate my nature. Many matador-alike car aves elucidated a dare to somebody set upon a hari-kari demise fate. Merely hop over a sideline to be set amid a busy lane? Somebody'd execute his anatomy by so pat a move.

But it, a move to have some car execute me, vilely roped in a car operator, a man or a woman of anonymity, fine life future, regular amity: somebody to have no desire to bedevil, execute, mop up, et. al., anybody. No, were my fate to be decided in a hari-kari fit, I'd isolate my rites of exile to demise.

So now, I was in a here-nor-a-yon-of-a-here to decide how I'd operate my new alive life. To begin, I revisited iter one-ninety-nine, to reset as I'd abided, in a pelota game to go by car utility tab. As I heretofore had it, a date became gone. No ride came, but I did operate to cop a few ecu-like dinero mites of a metal I figured as a token of amity hope. Dimes of a timely nature, cumulative to give me some beverage, were my pub ave for an ale bit of an amenity.

Todate, my divinity mates one more time sat. One minigod even arose to get an ale for everybody, so my fare was O.K. I was, as I had a sip, one yet in a demi-zone: not of a famine rage but of a desire for a bit of a cud.

I hesitate to relate how anybody ran on in amity, for it aped a similarity to my heretofore tale, to redo. Repetitive was a modify vocabulary fate to live by here: same site, same divinity mates. One more divinity delivered a beverage bonus of ale for everybody, so by time to go, my repose came facilely, fit as I was one more time to be put in a bag. I hesitated awarely to relate my dates of a date to come, for a future became more same. To wit, every date my game rode, but every ride to go became gone, to go by, so my time to revisit ale became some ceremony. No fare did I have but ale. Like some fabulosity tales aver, I was in a zone for a magical amen.

As every date became likewise, my hope was I had a duty to be here for a fate to be decided. One date, fate came.

Some car of a make for a model I had a memory to fit as one my life had one time decades ago, came to hesitate: Malibu. My Malibu had exuded a similar imagery, faded in a patina by sere mud of a ruby mire to cover a level enured in a toned analogy to some sun alit anew upon a horizon in a haze to mute color. It even abided in a zone my life had alit in: Oregon. A typical edit of a deposit eked one more patina layer over any viridity face, so my visibility was unawarely wary to note some man or a woman operator. I was even unaware to note how I was in a rite to behave. Did it abate for a rider or a beverage?

As it iterated a tap-a-tap-a-tap-a-tap-a rev, I decided it evoked a ride. To deliberate was a rude habit of any rider. I had a duty to get in.

As I did, I saw in awe: he was I.

So here we were, Daves, ex-I Dave to me, now as exiled-I Dave. Somehow, I was aware we were not on a pace to make tiny gab. If a rider is one to give his itinerary to some generosity delegate car operator, I had a duty to define my ride desire, but I saw evocatively Dave was as I was in on it.

As I was one beside my sole solidarity to be, my role was a given, as it operatively gave to be. But I yet imagined an elucidated ado was in a future he, we, had a duty to make now as one.

"How are we set in age? Mimical Ecole Parole?"

"How is it I relate to later?"

I come here to recapitulate my tales of a time gone by, so time to come can abovemore not erase color of any line made by man or any fine fabulosity done by us or anybody.

HERODOTUS

I lived in Oregon at a time before my Marine Base Conovowel era. For a Herodotus ave to set us up in a memory here made me cogitate how I had a military life to have lived, even if I were not in any legitimate war. Or even if I'd imagined it. As one to recapitulate lives of anybody, pal or enemy, Herodotus arose to have some fine facility to bury my fate's anatomical academic edit in a tome.

We (my Dave, me) lived in a Pacific idyl on a dune by water. I/ we were to finalize my paper on operative conovocality, some novel imaginary novel of a paper if I/ we were to be given an A-rated exonerated amen of a type to give me my BA/ MA. Had I, me, we, he finalized it ever? I, like many, had a repetitive reve: to be wakened as one naked in an exam, amid everybody covered, as I was alone not one to have done my labor.

As I/ we rode to vacate Califoregon in a time to go home to Pacific Oregon, ex-I Dave began an exegesis of a tale to relate how I/ we were here now.

"I was on a deliberate pace to be done, to do my paper as I had a duty to do before more came to be mine to do. But as I alit upon it in a fury to go for it, I became fused in a con of a desire to vary. To vary was operatively how it elucidated. It, as in a conovowel exegesis.

"I came to some divide to make my life go more yon or in a more here line, to become some military man or one to defy regimes of a military nature. Were my pose merely here to hesitate, my life'd arise to fix a ride to go, but as I meditated on a future for anybody, my life set up a maze to make some conovocalizer one to face many fixes of a nature to pose more to do.

"So, to fix it, as I revised a paper as I did a life to come, my M.O. was one to meditate by medicated ah. I made my body mimic a laboratory, to vary by medicinal ekes of anodyne doses of a cap used in a veterinary regime. A canine doc amigo gave me dose vices of a fine many types. As a vice, veterinary medicine ruled. Anyhow, I refined a move to become gone by medicated awe, like somebody can arise by nap in a reve to have.

"But it, as a regime, came to do nada. My fixes eliminated any solitary fix, as every decisive node became polymodal.

"At any rate, my paper abated. I had a fate to defer any tutored aside line. My para/ military life had a duty to begin. If I were to begin a gig as a marine, however, I had an abovemore desire to revise my life by paper at a date later. I led a bi-life, divided as one to vary by poses of every type. So duped, I became wise, somehow. I made my lives over, in an imaginary mica maze, so however I was, I was in a polymono modality. My literary life became literal; or, in a vice-varicose durability, my literary life came to make my literal episodes evoke literary tales.

"As it operated, I made my sidepal an imaginary literality. So here we were, side-by-side for a bit in a move to resonate. But as I developed it, it iterated an imaginary me to make his I.D. on a separate line, to develop a new abided abode. Somehow I figured I had a duty to refit us, united as one to be me, before we were done. To be done, by my paper, arose to become resolute to fix every fix I was ever in."

"If I can ahem a haw of a care to deliberate for a bit," I began, aware how I was evasive to debate my very time to live. "How is it I am? Am I merely some man imagined? Or am I verily here?"

"Can anybody verify his anatomy verily? Verily, we vary, to go here, yon. I nominate we, but I named us as one to be we. Never are we more fixed in a verity to be set as, on average, we become fixed in a verity to vary here. But it is, as I/ we noted, a bit of an agony to go forever in a waver. I move to fix it."

"I'm in an avidity to become fixed, as I've come to beg every divinity to do. Puny divinity types, even."

Ex-I Dave gave me some bit of a pat, in a move to revise to have made me come here: he revised it, as in a time to fix a finality, he had an avidity to finalize his one-time paper of Ecole Parole, to be done to go.

"So, we're merely here to go," my basic ability to make do was one to make sure. Hari-kari was a legalized Oregon utility, but a lot of executive rules regulated it if anybody desired a demise by law. "Are we to be done by demise?"

"No, not in a literal iterated exegesis, as I get it." Ex-I Dave did elaborate. "We have no regular anatomy to finalize by demise."

"So we have come to be set up as imaginary."

"Yes or as one devised. 'Imagined' or 'imaginary' cajoles an image to make do by reve. We're more devised, as in operatively deduced in a logic of a rule-based itinerary."

"Fine. Have we herefore resolutely fixed it? Are we to be done? How?"

"As I/ we put in a paper, as I/ we type, we're to be fixed as it is."

Ex-I Dave figured it as I figured, even if an omen agitated a negative vibe. But if I were he, we were to be fixed, as in united. One had a duty to go forever in a unit? I figured I was in one, but even if I'd aver a desire to be done, now I wavered.

As one to be some demi-side human of an imaginary me, Dave was aware how I wavered.

"In one validity, we're set in an inability to vary how it is as a verity to go. We have no role but one to be set in a verity my paper operates. A rule role to go forever."

As ex-I Dave generated a velocity by Malibu to deliver us on a ride to some Pacific Oregon abode to labor on a paper I solely had a memory to reset, I relaxed. I gazed at a vegetative viridity gone but in an ebony set of a sun aloha we raced in a vanity to mimic any celerity. Miles of a widely ravaged arena to facilitate some log economy made for a motive to cut a fir ecology zone to put us on a line to Dune City.

*

We came to be set in a hut aside dunes on a site by some humanity-made lake far afar, as afar as any watery Pacific abided in a hereby locale. We had aromas of a saline nature to refer evocatively to lido life, but any visibility to verify water a là nature in a locale hereby was AWOL.

It was eleven. Ex-I Dave let us in. An ice box amid a culinary recovery cove had a six of a rude lager of amenity to give, so we made for it, every bit of it, in a repose to demobilize.

Dave had an academy token of a salary to take for a time. He'd arisen as an examiner of a TA type tutor. A tiny nut of a pile to have, his elusive salary made do here.

Dune City he defined as a nice locality for one to do some job of an academy mop-up. Every date, he got up in a fury to get it over. Every date, he'd abate. He had a desire for a muse to relate how a tome came to be done. Herefore, he had, as one resolute to do duty, come to locate me. Side-by-side, we'd operate, yoked as oxen.

As an ox of a muse to motivate him, I was in a daze, but I liked it, on average, to be let in on it. I was of a desire to nap, as one tired of a ride to be rid of. As I made for a bed, ex-I Dave posed a muse role for exile-me Dave to take.

"Give me some reve to go by, some reve to make me relate my paper."

I was agog in a daze to defy him, as I had an avidity to relax. I was, if of any pat ability, wired evocatively to give him a reve, however. As ex-I Dave got in a bed, I bowed.

A sofa hereby became my base to generate waves of a reve to give Dave his ah of a ha. He was, in a jif, in a doze to saw a log as every hale haled. I gave my muse gig a go, but I was of a debility to generate. To simulate some generated edit, I decided I'd open a side gap of evocativity.

Here was a televisor. I put it on, as one bored arises in a fit of inanity to do. Wired on a line to some hereby net, it operated on a tiny gamut of a wave-set agility to give locales of an amenity fare. Solely five wave-locales of amenity were here to have. Locales eleven, one, five gave notes of a local utility nature (time, city rules, any bake sales). A remote locale seven alit upon a hazily wavy far afar ozone to defer any visibility. Locale nine was a cinema lode. Given a debility to vary, my desire was as one fixed.

At any rate, we were set up O.K.

"O, Toto, here's a site like home!" came by line to forebode cinematic inimitability.

But it aped as a remake—not an Oz of any fit ability.

Never-a-more, here were some similarity zones of a type to make my faked Oz one to be doted upon.

A Vizir of Oz alit in a Saraha-like zone. To refine repetitively some model of a cinematic ah, a maker of opuses of an Oz-originated evocativity had executed it, as one beside some more. To name but a few: *A Maven of Oz, A Magus of Oz, A Bonus of Oz, A Boner of Oz* (one to poke fun at Oz opuses in a jocular erotica parody). For a time here, Locale Nine put on a fete to honor every copy but *A Boner of Oz*, as any boner arose to rile civility by rites of a fine many tidily definitive sex episodes.

Anyhow, *A Vizir of Oz* emulated a model of original Oz, as it awoke some rote tale. To wit, a locale gave many rube caricatures of amity, levity, regularity to regale some gal of an age to be tutored in imaginative lore. Some delivered edibility fare, some made ceramic adobes, one was a camel operator, et. al. Any gal, even a rube, became bored in a rural arena. So bored as one to hope to vary how it operated.

One fateful eve, some huge gale generated a calamity hubub, as everybody ran in avidity to be covered. Everybody but one gal, a Dora. Dora was on a job of utility, beside her animal, a kid of a pet of a name Toto, to get enumerative dates, in a repetitive gig a gal of a Sahara-like zone had a duty to do. Her evocative hopes of a desire to vary had operatively made her a focus of a calamity made by her.

As ebony came to cover every bit of a hover up above, some tube-like cumulus of a fury piped an anemosity to remove Dora, Toto far afar.

In a para-set arena, Dora, Toto woke to be put in a revery to figure how anybody was in a role here. By-to-by, Dora met one man, one more man, a woman, et. al., of a fabulosity to be metahuman, as everybody was a caricature to be somebody holy, demonic, or of a desire to be saved in one life to some more lifelike life. Some serenaded a musical ode to relate some desire to fix a malady, set-up, et. al.

> As in:
> If I were some rex of a city
> Not a dupe, not a dope, but a rex.

> Or:
> If I merely had a cereb
> I'd imagine to figure
> Cogitate to deliver
> If I merely had a cereb.

Episodes elucidated a tale to take Dora, Toto to some demonic abode to be bedeviled as every caricature had a fate to be, til a holy-like Vizir exuded a hope for any to become saved if any came to have him as an elite ruler. As afar as one Dora was in a desire be here, her exile rode to bore her one more time. Set-up in a futility to be done, Dora solely desired an exit on a ride to go home.

To do so became basic as a fate to hope for. A Vizir of Oz or any zone was a mere man of an imitator in a holy role. Dora, Toto had a time to figure him as a fake vizir. As Ozy generated a gale-like hubub in a move to make her agog, agile Toto bit a bit of a robe he wore, to make him abate his awesome hubub in a yap of agony.

So, to get everybody to go, he gave her ululated ekes of a volubility to have power over a mobility to go home.

Haze came to take her. In a bit of an aha, Dora woke, to be home, put in a bed. Everybody Dora had a memory to have for a relative, pal, or an enemy was aside her, even agile Toto, set in original evocative caricature to populate her arenas arena. Boredom eluded every care for a gal in an amity to be reset in a zone sanity gave her.

"O, Toto, here's a site like home."

"Hit it, Omar," a relative made music arise for a tune Dora had a tone to do.

> So far over a nova
> So far on
> It is a site to go for
> One time to be so gone.

To go far up a nova
Fates are fine
Reves I'd ever imagine
Merely to verify.

Some date my hopes upon a sun
Are sure to waken every fun
Aside me.
Here cares evaporate like haze
For every dare beset to faze.
So come to ride me.

So far over a nova
Some dare ride.
Some get over a nova
So how-o-come can I?

Some get it on upon a nova
So how-o-come can I?

*

We wakened anew in a new abode. Dave by bed aside me by sofa. Pale sonic ado by televized aloha saturated every node. Famines in unanimity set us on a peripatetic exit of a hike to go to Dune City, to be fed in a diner. In a mile, here we were.

Dave had imagined an ah of a ha came to him in a magical ave by reve made by me, so my role here was one not in any mode to defy. He merely had a cinematic inoculum of a reve-like hypo-poked eke give notice to him of a desire to take to do his academy duty. How I was aware? He vocalized a tune by hum. I noted one melody, more, by likened imitative tones, even if ex-I Dave had a typical inability to hit a note. Some sub of a liminal ability he did execute, to have taken in Oz as if in a reve.

"To put it over," ex-I Dave became revelatory, "we posit an as-if Oz of a para-verisimilitude set-up in one zone to verify some meta-zone."

He was agog as any zany po-mo bozo, but I let an academy mule vocabulary degenerate to lucidity for a man in a fire to get a tome done. Besides, I was aware how it operated, as I was or I had arisen as ex-I-Dave. But in any case, was anybody not up on Oz? As a cinematic opera for anybody to refer evocatively to for an analogical exegesis, Oz exuded a wide capacity to be modeled.

As a bicipital unit of a sane fit or as one gone loco solo, we'd analogize Dune City, every citizen or any visitor alive here to populate some para-here to populate my paper. Even in a locale made by namesake dunes, a city here had a Sahara side to rival any Delaware pit of an edifice mine. We were liberated. Every caricature capitalized on an analogy jag of a morality solely made by conovowel, a motive to take however any vocabulary came to volubility, by rote note, lyrical ode, demotic

American usages, esoteric academic abuses of any to every type to be typed in a paper of a tome to bury me.

Bury me? Yes. I was one to be done, but one to be put in a tome done line-by-line, to live forever (if in a paper on a paper of a non-acidity nature). Nowadate, we had, abovemore, bytes of a capacity to locate forever any paper in a database, so my life had a future, so to put it, even if I were done.

We sat at a bar in a diner operated as a café for a matinal edacity. Later, it operated as a bar of a bar. At one side, some riser of a mesa had a mic, as it arose to be made to be some type cabaret. A lined aloha bade, "Tonite! Revival aces OnoxonO!"

"Some cover unit," elucidated ex-I Dave. "Like live kara-yodel or American Idol."

As an "Amana," by tag of a name, delivered a java recap, I had a desire to revisit one more denizen I was aware to have had as a pal. As I gazed, I saw a gamut of a many likely caricatures: one to be some fop, one to some to be pirates, a woman of anatomy bevy, men of every race but one.

But aha! Beside me sat a lad of an avidity to peruse some comic. A luridity cover in a five color awe came to generate power of a lure. Lines of a huge type waved in a likewise fury to make love to war in a savage *Tora Tora Tora!* to befit a Japanese marine, done tete-to-tip in a military get-up, as one to bayonet an enemy to be but a hero. He, my hero but enemy, was a man of a time gone by, made to saturate motives of a lad of avidity to have.

"Can a tuna can a tuna," my bow arose to rile my lad of a rube. He made some face to relegate me to degenerate level.

Ex-I-Dave got a pen as one to take notes, as evocatively he came to liberate me.

"Relax, it's over."

Doug Nufer is the author of the novels *Negativeland* (Autonomedia, 2004), *Never Again* (Black Square, 2004), *On the Roast* (Chiasmus, 2004), *The Mudflat Man/ The River Boys* (soultheft records, 2006), and *By Kelman Out of Pessoa* (Les Figues, 2011). His books of poetry include *We Were Werewolves* (Make Now, 2008), *The Dammed* (ubu.com, 2011), and *Lounge Acts* (Insert Blanc, 2013).

Louis Bury is the author of *Exercises in Criticism* (Dalkey Archive, 2015).

9 781941 550434